SECRETS OF SPARROW HALL

A CHILDREN'S MYSTERY ADVENTURE

BRENDA LARKIN

HULLABALOO PUBLISHING

To Camille Alexandria
with love

CONTENTS

Title Page

Copyright

Dedication

Introduction

1 GILL MOSS   3

2 DOG AND GUN   16

3 MAB AND THE FIR TREES   29

4 CRAVEN WOOD   40

5 CROXTETH HALL   48

6 MONKS DOWN   55

7 SEDGE MOOR   65

8 HALL BROOK   71

9 STONE BRIDGE   77

10 SPARROW HALL   83

About The Author   99

INTRODUCTION

TYUS and SEREN, brother and sister, time travel once again. This time it is 1798.

LIVERPOOL is now a thriving port and the population is growing but the villages on the edges of the city are surrounded by countryside.

GILL MOSS is an area of dairy and vegetable farming. It is home to JOE KIRKBY and a secret Catholic chapel hidden beneath the loft of the farmhouse where he lives.

THE DOG AND GUN is a tavern nearby. It is a gathering place for NED LEWIS and his poaching gang – WILL, OLD TOM, MATTY, MARIE.

CROXTETH HALL is a large country house and estate owned by the Molyneux family. In 1798, WILLIAM Philip Molyneux is the 2nd EARL OF SEFTON. The grounds are extensive and plentiful with deer and wildlife, which attracts the poachers.

THE FRENCH REVOLUTION began in 1789 and led to the execution of Louis XVI and Marie Antoinette in 1793. The surviving members of the French royal family escaped to other parts of Europe. CHARLES, COUNT OF ARTOIS (COMTE D'ARTOIS), who later became KING CHARLES X, was given shelter in Britain. Often he would visit his friend, WILLIAM, EARL OF SEFTON at Croxteth Hall with his attendants, the Baron of ROLLES and the Duke of

BERRY.
CHEF BALAND and his daughter THERESE accompany them.

SPARROW HALL is the home of CAPTAIN RANWORTH, sea captain, explorer and gentleman.

THE PUZZLES

Each chapter begins with a word puzzle whose solutions taken together will reveal Tyus and Seren's mission and another SECRET OF SPARROW HALL.

Answers at the end of our tale.

MAP OF OLD GILL MOSS AND CROXTETH

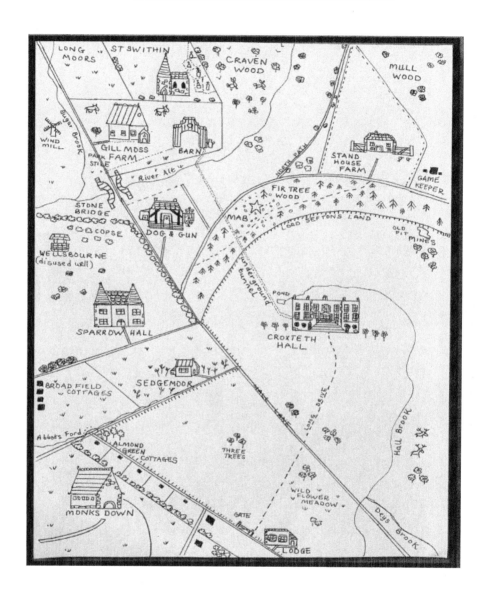

1 GILL MOSS

Are we not drawn inward, we few, drawn inward to new erA

Seren lay flat and put her ear to the ground. She was sure she had heard a sound – a metallic clang or a dull thump. She remembered reading that Native American tribes were able to hear the hoof beats of small groups of horses vibrating through the ground from miles away, by listening to the earth.

She was lying on the floor of the pantry in the Old Mill house, her home for a year now. It was from this room she and her brother Tyus had followed lights beneath a trap door, which had led them through a tunnel and into a land that existed over a thousand years earlier in the Middle Ages.

It was from there they had rescued their father who had been imprisoned in a medieval castle and now the family was living happily together back in the present. But it was difficult to forget the exciting adventure they had had, the people and animals they had met, especially Rufus, the scent hound, who had guided them through the magical land. Seren often thought she would like to see them again.

She wondered about the other people they had rescued known as The Whisperers. Did they make it back to their own time? She hoped they were as happy as her family.

Tyus creaked open the door and shook his head.

'It's over, Seren. The trap door has gone and Dad is home.'

He rapped on the floor with a rat-a-tat-tat.

'We're not going back.'

Seren pursed her lips. It was not the first time Tyus had reprimanded her. He often found her sitting quietly in the pantry. She blinked up at him.

'I heard something, Ty. I know it!'

'Probably the water pipes. The house is ancient; it creaks and groans like a hundred year old man,' he laughed.

'Ugh! That doesn't make me feel better. That sounds creepy.' She stood up quickly and shivered.

'I'm going for dinner. I suppose Mum asked you to fetch me?' she said leaving the room with a skip.

Tyus waited until she had gone before he closed the door and stamped on the floor himself. The trap door had disappeared and everything was back to normal. He knelt down and listened – nothing, no sound. To be extra certain he stretched out and pressed his ear to the floorboards – silence. He grinned. Exactly the sound he needed to hear. Scrambling to his feet relieved, he opened the door and switched off the light and there it was – CLANG!

Flicking the light back on, he waited a moment – CLANG!

There was definitely a sound. He shrugged his shoulders and switched off the light, making sure the door was firmly closed.

Pipes, water pipes, central heating, that's what I heard, nothing else. No need to tell Seren she was right.

Tyus smiled wanly through dinner but hardly uttered a word. He imagined, at any second, the clanging would start and everyone would hear but it seemed to have stopped. It was his favourite meal though; pasta followed by ice cream, so no one noticed his silence. Everyone was thinking he was enjoying his food too much to talk, he presumed. Mum was chatting away. It was almost a year since she had opened her dance studio and she had been making preparations for a huge concert and party celebration in the village hall, which was taking place tomorrow. She was so excited. The dance classes had been a huge success and the business was thriving. But more importantly, she was happy to be doing what she had always longed to do since she was young. Her dream had come true. Everything was set up for the party; bunting, balloons, tables and costumes for the special show were in place. The Lord Mayor and other special guests had been invited. It was going to be amazing.

Dad was back at work and in his spare time was ready to help at the dance school with scenery or odd jobs. He was content and grateful to be back with his family He had never revealed to Loria where he had been and explained his mysterious disappearance by saying he had lost his memory. Loria was too happy to delve further into the story.

He discussed it with Tyus and Seren. No one would believe them, especially their Mum, if they revealed they had rescued him from the evil Commissioners along with other prisoners known as The Whisperers, by travelling through time! All agreed it was safer to stick to the loss of memory story.

Tyus was enjoying the family back together. He didn't want to hear clanging noises from the pantry or tell Seren he had heard them too. He stole a quick glance at her during dinner, worried in case she could read his thoughts but she was happily munching her second slice of garlic bread, oblivious to him.

Then Mum got a text on her mobile phone, and another. Everyone could hear the pings from the other room. She always left her phone in there while they were eating. It was a rule she had – no phones or tablets, no tech at the table.

Then the house phone rang which was very unusual and caused

everyone to freeze a moment. Dad picked it up. No one moved as they watched his brow furrow and his eyes narrow. He put down the receiver and assessed his family's concerned faces.

'Loria, it's all right,' he began calmly, 'no one has been hurt but there's a fire at the Village Hall. The fire engines are there now.'

'Oh no! A fire!' Loria pressed her hand against her mouth. She stood up then sat down again immediately.

'Everyone's fine?' she asked.

Dad assured her that no one was in the building at the time. She checked her phone. She scrolled through the messages from friends alerting her to the fire and asking if everything was well. Her eyes scanned the texts quickly.

'We have to go into the village to see the damage,' she decided. 'But Tyus, Seren, I want you to stay here. Dad and I won't be long. It's only a few minutes away.'

Dad turned to the children, his jaw set firmly.

'Will you be all right for half an hour while we check this out?'

He grabbed his car keys.

'Yes, of course,' Seren replied, 'don't worry about us.'

'We'll be fine,' added Tyus, 'Just go! See what's happened.'

'Look after your sister, Tyus.' Mum squeezed them both.

There was no more to be said. Tyus and Seren watched as their parents drove off down the road into the village. A plume of smoke could be seen above the rooftops, curling upwards towards the waiting grey clouds.

Back in the kitchen, Seren began clearing away the dinner plates.

'A fire, a fire in the village hall!' she gasped. 'That's one of the oldest buildings here. It must be over two hundred years old.'

Tyus carried the heavier serving dishes into the kitchen.

'Poor Mum, all her party stuff is in there.'

He carefully placed the bowls on the side wondering if he should attempt to wash them or load them in the dishwasher. His thoughts were abruptly interrupted because that's when the clanging and the thumping began in earnest from the pantry room. It was next door to the kitchen and the sound reverberated round the kitchen walls, becoming louder and louder each time there was a clang. The appliances and everything made from metal in the kitchen were crashing and banging together, joining in with the beat. It became even louder. The children covered their ears. As the cacophony reached a crescendo, the pantry room door flew open. Then the ringing stopped.

Seren giggled. Her eyes widened.

'Did you hear the noise that time?'

'It's not funny Seren. That was scary.' Tyus gulped.

'We have to look, Ty,' Seren said as she approached the door and peeked inside. The trap door was back! This time it was open, gaping like the entrance to Aladdin's cave and was lit from beneath. The light beamed up onto the pantry ceiling bathing the room in a cool glow.

Seren folded her arms waiting for Tyus's assessment. He frowned.

'I don't think we should go back Seren. Dad is home safe now. If we go into the tunnel, we have no idea what will happen. It could be dangerous.'

'There must be a reason why the trap door has appeared again and what are those noises? I think we should investigate.' She saw his lips curl. 'Look, if it's dangerous we'll come back at once.'

CLANG!

'Let's see what the noise is at least,' Seren pleaded but she didn't wait for his answer.

She slipped her legs across the opening and found the rungs of the ladder with her feet. She moved backwards down the first few steps to the passageway beneath. The light went out.

Tyus gave an exasperated sigh. 'Seren! Wait!'

Too late, Seren was already walking along the tunnel. Her voice was echoing.

'I'm going even if you're not.'

Tyus took a torch from the pantry shelf and muttering to himself about promises and mothers, scrambled down the ladder after his sister. He shone the torch along the winding passageway. It curved and twisted almost back on itself. Last time they went into the tunnel, the walls were dark and wet, moist with moss and dew; this time the tunnel walls were stronger and speckled with small stones and pebbles, which caught the light from his torch and glistened. He followed the torchlight along the snaking passage until he found Seren. Her shadow spread out against the tunnel walls and licked up the sides and onto the ceiling. She spun round and waved.

'I see daylight ahead. There's an entrance.'

Tyus caught up with her. He was still cross.

'I'm only here because I promised Mum. I don't think it's a good idea and if anything happens...'

'I know,' she admitted, 'It will be my fault. But thanks for coming. Let's take a peek, that's all.'

She gave him one of her mischievous smiles, which he recognized at once and which made it impossible for him to stay cross with her.

CLANG!

They both jumped suddenly. It was close. Tyus switched off the torch and without another word they moved stealthily towards the entrance. He held up his hand to stop Seren and pointed at himself with his thumb. Seren nodded. He would investigate first.

The first thing he noticed was they were in a barn and the doors were open wide. The barn itself was empty except for a wooden cart with two enormous wheels at the rear and long protruding sticks at the front, which would attach it to a horse. In the cart were tall, metal, conical shaped containers with handles on the sides. Some more containers were lying by the open door and some were lined up on a stand by the cart. It was quiet again.

Seren and Tyus stepped gingerly on to the straw floor and walked around the cart. Seren tapped the side of a container. It made the metallic, hollow clanging sound they had been hearing.

CLANG!

Objects near the door were being lifted and dropped by someone unseen. They banged into each other with a clunk. Then a boy appeared, rolling them into the barn and kicking at them angrily with his boots.

Seren and Tyus hid behind the cart and watched the boy. He was about nine or ten, and dressed in ragged clothing. He heaved the empty cylinders into the barn. He brushed away the floppy fringe of his long, untidy brown hair with his hand and sat on the straw. It was then the children could see he was crying.

He sobbed loudly with his head in his hands, loud, gasping sobs. He came up for the occasional gulp of air, rubbed his eyes then wept some more. After a while he stopped, exhausted and lay back on the straw and stared up at the roof of the barn. Rays of sunlight found their way through the gaps in the roof and lit up his face. His eyes were chestnut brown and his cheeks were grubby with the sun and the crying. Although he was young, he looked strong and wiry as if he were used to hard work like moving heavy cylinders about.

'What shall we do?' whispered Seren.

Tyus raised his eyebrows.

'Now we've seen who was making the noise – are you ready to go back like you said?'

Seren took a deep breath.

'He looks so sad. What do *you* want to do? Shall we go back into the tunnel and leave him?'

She glanced across to the corner of the barn where they had come through the tunnel. The opening was still there. They had a chance to return and not get involved with the sad, angry boy.

'Come on,' said Tyus standing up and pulling his sister up from her kneeling position, "Let's go... and help him!'

Tyus stepped forward and coughed.

'Hello, are you all right?'

The boy shot to his feet in a flash. He bowed his head low and looked more embarrassed than alarmed.

'Please don't be frightened, my brother and I only want to help.'

Hearing Seren's soft voice, he raised his head and rubbed his cheeks mixing his tears in with the dirt on his face.

'I am well, kind mistress and master. Forgive my outburst. It is unbecoming of me.'

'You're upset,' said Seren coaxing more information from him.

'It is nothing, Milady for you to be troubled. I have to attend to a task that I am unhappy about but I must obey Farmer Langley.'

'Who is he?' asked Tyus.

The boy seemed genuinely surprised.

'Why, he is the farmer who tenants the land for you. Who herds the cows for you and provides milk for the Hall and all surrounding villages. Farmer Langley runs the dairy farm for all of the Gill Moss.'

'And who are you?' followed up Seren smiling.

'I am a button, Milady, a gnat, a lowly farm worker, helping to move these churns here on to the cart, to deliver to yourselves up at the great Hall.'

Seren laughed. He thought they were landed gentry or living in a fine mansion. Perhaps it was her sequin dance top and colourful skirt she was wearing that made her appear rich or Tyus's new smart tracksuit that gave him a sleek air of importance.

'What is your real name?' pressed Tyus. 'Do you have one?'

The boy straightened his clothing and stood tall.

'Sir, my name is Joe, Joseph Kirkby. I am at your service. I am sorry I did not see you arrive from the underground tunnel. Please allow me to escort you to the secret room.'

'Wait Joe, we are not here to see a secret room and you don't have to call us milady or sir, I'm Seren,' Seren said kindly.

'And I'm Tyus. We want to know if we can help before we go back home. Tell us why you are crying and making all the noise throwing milk churns around?'

'And,' joined in Seren, 'how did you know about the tunnel?'

Joe tipped his head to one side and scratched it. The high borns at the manor don't usually stop to talk to the likes of him. He had seen several of the Earl's family coming through the secret underground tunnel that led from the Hall to the dairy stables. If they came at night, he would take a lantern and lead them through the courtyard and into the cottage nearby.

Farmer Langley lived in the front part of the cottage and presented a normal everyday appearance to the officers of the law, while he left it to Joe to take the risks in smuggling the family members or visiting noblemen staying with the Earl, up to the secret room at the top of the farmhouse. The secret room was a Catholic chapel.

It had been dangerous times for Catholics at the Hall and in England. The Molyneux family, from the Great Hall at Croxteth, had been secretly Catholic and although it was forbidden, the old Earl had arranged for a chapel to be built in the loft of the farmhouse at Gill Moss for the family to pray in secret. A tunnel was built from the Hall to the dairy farm. Often, the old Earl and senior members of his household would come to pray. Even though times were improving, it was 1798 and illegal for priests to celebrate Mass and for people to gather for Catholic prayers. There was a new Earl now but he never attended as he was no longer a Catholic but if he had Catholic guests staying, they could secretly pray at services in the secret chapel.

Tyus and Seren knew nothing of this. Their tunnel from the Mill House and the Hall tunnel had merged to bring them to Gill Moss.

Joe thought for a moment. He had heard French noblemen were

staying at the Hall, but these children were not French and they were not wearing the Moline shaped cross of the Molyneux family on their clothes, so who were they? He took a closer look at the new visitors. Suddenly, they appeared different, not like the Earl's family and not like servants from the household. Their clothing was odd. They spoke kindly enough but with a strange directness. They were unfamiliar with the secret room - surely if they were from the Hall they would know it was a chapel. Also, it was the wrong time of day. The priest was not here. Farmer Langley, who was strict about such comings and goings, would have warned him to expect the priest and the faithful.

In fact, the farmer had given him other instructions. He had given Joe a cruel and bitter task to perform, which was the cause of Joe's anger and was breaking his heart.

Joe took a step back, then another. He picked up one of the milk churns ready to throw at them.

'Who are you?' he challenged. 'You're not from the Hall!'

'Hey, a minute please Joe.' Tyus pushed Seren behind the cart. 'Stand back, Seren!'

'Please don't hurt us Joe, we want to help.' Seren called from behind the spokes of the large wooden wheel of the cart.

Joe swung round to face Tyus.

'Don't come a step nearer, are you ghosts a haunting me?'

'No,' said Tyus, 'we're children just like you. I'm eleven and my sister is nine. We came here another way, that's all. We heard the milk churns banging and came to see but if you don't want our help, we will return home.'

Joe let the milk churn drop onto the ground. Clang! Although it was empty, it was heavy when raised above the head. Seren edged nearer.

'You were very upset before. We saw you crying and kicking the milk churns about.'

Joe sat on the churn, his hands on his lap.

'There's nothing you can do. I have a task is all. Orders from Farmer Langley.'

'We can leave or you can tell us about it. It's up to you,' said Tyus.

'And we are definitely not ghosts,' smiled Seren.

Joe smiled back ruefully.

'I will tell but there's nothing to be done.'

He glanced back over his shoulder into the farmyard and gestured with his hand.

'It's my dog. Well, the farm's dog. He's my only friend. We go everywhere together and he's been at my side for as long as I can remember.'

Tyus and Seren listened carefully.

'Farmer Langley was playing cards up at the tavern with Ned and was on a losing streak but that didn't stop him betting.'

Joe kicked the churn again.

'He used the dog as a stake and lost. Now he is sending me to the tavern to hand him over to Ned.' Joe gulped.

'And that's not the worst of it. Ned Lewis and his men are poachers. They hunt and steal from the lands round here. Because our dog is a sight and scent hound, he's expensive. They've been after him for years. It be so cruel to ask me to hand him over knowing how much he means to me.'

Joe wiped another huge tear.

'Did you say scent hound?' asked Seren.

'Aye, yes, he's outside tied up. Come see, meet him, I call him Rufus.'

2 DOG AND GUN

(UNSCRAMBLE THE ANAGRAM)
SILENT READ EARTH

'Rufus!' Tyus and Seren both cried out.

'It can't be,' said Tyus.

They ran from the barn into the open air and across the farmyard. Chickens, pecking for food, leapt from their path. A stone cottage stood apart from the barn. Its walls were whitewashed and a lantern was fixed above the doorway. The roof was thatched and steep, which was where the secret room and the chapel lay. Behind the cottage, a cobbled path led through a graveyard. Lichen and moss grew on the tombstones and the disused chapel of St Swithin, with boarded up windows, sat gloomily in the distance. The chapel was built long ago in 1410 but had been shut down for thirty years. Wild flowers grew, entwining the porch with dog roses and daisies. Tied up in front of the farmhouse door was a golden haired hound. He was curled up with his head resting on his front paws. His fur was long and shaggy like their dear friend Rufus who had helped them rescue their father and the Whisperers, the last time they travelled through the time tunnel.

But could it be him?

That time seemed centuries before this one. Then, the land

they travelled to consisted of open fields with very few buildings. Now, there were stately homes, stone cottages, horses and carts, barns and underground tunnels. It couldn't be Rufus. He would have to be centuries old. Perhaps it was a descendent of Rufus – his great, great, great, grand pup?

The dog saw them coming. His ears pricked up and his nose sniffed the air. He jumped excitedly, trying to run towards them but he was tethered to the gatepost. He barked a greeting. Joe reached him first and ruffled his neck.

'Down boy, you'll have old Farmer Langley out next. Come and meet my new friends.'

Tyus and Seren watched impatiently and with beating hearts as Joe untied the lead. They stared hard at the dog. He was like Rufus in every way. The hound broke free and bounded towards them, licking their faces. He stood on his hind legs to his full height and bumped Tyus's chest. Then he nuzzled Seren's neck like the old Rufus used to do.

'I've never seen him friendly like that to anyone before,' Joe said puzzled.

Seren hugged Rufus round his middle.

'I think we've met before though. This is a very special dog you have here, Joe.'

Tyus knelt down and patted Rufus along his warm back.

'How have you been Rufus, old chap? You know we missed you.'

'How...how do you know him? Is he your dog? Did you lose him?' Joe asked in a worried voice.

'Over here,' Tyus said leading Rufus away from the cottage out of earshot of Farmer Langley.

'He's not our dog exactly but there was a dog just like him and maybe this could be him, if dogs lived to be 800 years old! The dog we knew helped us when we were in danger.'

'I think that's why we've come back,' declared Seren. "I think he *is* the real Rufus and he needs our help now for whatever danger he is in.'

'How?' Joe gasped. 'Are you taking him from me? At least if he went to the poachers, I might see him about but if you take him, I'll never see him again.'

He stood in front of Rufus and crossed his arms. 'And I'd be punished for losing him. The poachers and Langley would both beat me.'

'Don't worry, Joe,' said Tyus, 'I'm not sure what we can do but we won't take Rufus from you. He's your dog now.'

'Maybe we can reason with the poachers? When are you taking him to them?' Seren asked.

'Right this moment. I'm taking him to the Dog and Gun Tavern, beyond the Stone Bridge. You could try but Ned is not one for parleying.'

He reattached the lead to Rufus and started walking along the stony path, past the meadow where the cows were grazing until next milking time and a willow tree surrounded by yellow gorse.

'Tell us about yourself, Joe. Don't you have parents?' asked Seren.

Joe looked straight ahead. Rufus was taking a drink from the brook.

'No, my parents died long ago. Farmer Langley's housekeeper looked after me but then she died. Langley kept me on as long as I say nothing and work at the farm.'

Seren said nothing but thought how sad and hard it must be for Joe. Reading her thoughts, Joe gave her a reassuring smile.

'Don't worry Miss Seren. When I'm older I'm going to leave here and sail the seas. The city is a thriving port and busy with ships from miles afar. The countryside ways are dying, everything is changing and I want to see the world.'

'That sounds like a good plan,' chuckled Tyus.

'But I wanted Rufus to come with me,' sighed Joe.

The lane turned on to a wider road with cottages either side. Their low doors opened out onto the dusty road. The new friends crossed the Stone Bridge, then more houses appeared and buildings – the largest of which had a colourful painted sign swinging outside, with the writing 'Dog and Gun.' There was a picture of a musket and a dog. A group of rough fellows saw them coming. One of them shouted into the tavern.

'The lad's here with the dog, Ned.'

'Send him in,' shouted a voice from the gloom inside the tavern.

'Step lively, mate,' one of the fellows ordered.

Joe adjusted the string around Rufus's neck and whispered into his ear.

'I'm sorry dear pal. If there was any other way...but your old friends Tyus and Seren, they say they can help, so trust us. We won't let any harm come to you.'

He stroked the hound's silky ears, 'Let's go!'

They entered the tavern. It was set out with a few tables inhabited by groups of men eating and drinking. Some were unwashed and unshaven; some were playing cards or staring into their drinks.

On an open fireplace, a woman was roasting a pig, turning the spit slowly so the juices sizzled onto the grate beneath. Occasionally, she stopped and cut a slice of its meat with a sharp knife and placed it into a bowl for a customer.

On the largest table, onlookers were gathered round amused by a game they were watching. Ned, the leader of the group, was winning. One of his followers, a young lad they called Will, was losing.

'Come on lad, it's not hard. Pick one! Where's the shrunken pea?'

Ned turned his head to the other men. He rubbed his hand over his stubbly beard and winked. Will was not distracted. He eyed three downturned walnut shells on the table. The pea was under one of them - but which? So far he hadn't chosen right, even though he never took his eyes off the shells. He stared at each shell in turn.

'Give me a minute. You never give me long enough to choose.'

'Will, my lad, I could travel to Sparrow Hall and back and you wouldn't have enough time!'

A well-dressed man sitting alone at a table by the window coughed loudly and plunged a knife into his meat
'I'll not have you anywhere near Sparrow Hall, Ned, nor any of your group of underhanded swindlers,' he said.

The man grimaced and waited for Ned's reply. Ned offered an oily smile and tried to make light of the comment.

'I didn't see you sitting there, Captain Ranworth, I was merely jesting. Sparrow Hall is a fine respectable house. I were using it as a marker. The boy you see, Will, he's very slow.'

Then turning to Will angrily, he shouted.

'I've lost my patience. Make your choice boy, double or nothing.'

The Captain scoffed and turned away. Now the odds were increased, Will felt under more pressure but Ned's piercing blue eyes unnerved him and made him make a snap decision. Will reached forward and picked up the middle shell.

It was empty. No pea was in sight. There was laughter and groans from the other poachers.

'Lost again, Will,' jeered one of them.

The children had been watching the scene with astonishment and had sensibly stayed out of the way until the game had ended. Ned stretched out his large arms taking the winnings from Will. It was only a few pennies but it was all Will had. Then Ned caught sight of Joe and Rufus.

'And now, here comes another prize. Bring him closer boy. The Langley dog, better than anyone could purchase at the Kennels.' Ned announced.

Joe gently tugged at the lead and slowly brought Rufus to Ned, glancing at Tyus and Seren, hoping they could do something to stop the handover.

'Wait!' said Tyus. 'You like a wager. I'll bet you I can find the pea under the walnut shell and we get to keep the dog.'

Ned was always ready to play the game with a newcomer – who knows what he could win - truth was, he never lost.

'And what could a slip of a lad have that I would want? Do you have money? Jewels? Silver?' He gave a lopsided grin. His cronies scoffed and laughed at their leader's joke.

Tyus took his key ring from his pocket and placed it on the table. It wasn't gold but it had gold plating around a shiny, black plastic disc. The tab was made from a marmalade coloured, fake crocodile print. It was different from anything they had seen before.

'What is this?' growled Ned, 'Gold? Onyx? Crocodile skin?

Where did you get this treasure?'

The words brought Captain Ranworth to the table to investigate.

'Let me see. I'll vouch if it is of any value.'

Immediately, Ned and his companions stepped back allowing Captain Ranworth plenty of space to study the strange object. The Captain held the key ring in the palm of his hand. He flipped it over and ran his fingers over the 'crocodile' skin. He felt the weight of it in his hand. He turned to Tyus.

'Where did you get this boy? Have you been travelling?'

His face was handsome and his voice strong but kind, not like the way he had spoken to Ned.

'It's mine,' said Tyus worried he would know they were time travelling. 'Let me guess which shell has the pea and win the dog.'

Captain Ranworth's eyes sought out the dog that was so important. Seren and Joe were sitting with Rufus, patting him gently to keep him calm. The Captain placed the key ring on the table.

'It's real,' he said. 'It has value more than the hound. If I were you Ned Lewis, I'd risk another play.'

Tyus sighed. The Captain stood by the side of the table.

'But I'm standing here to make sure there's no cheating.'

'I'm no cheat!' Ned protested but all his comrades' faces declared that they suspected Ned always won by cheating. No one had eyes fast enough to see how he did it and no one dared say it.

When Ned placed the pea under one of the shells and shuffled them, he was so fast; no one could see him palm the pea. Then he palmed it back on to the table afterwards. He was too clever for them. Will scrunched up his face as he suspected he might have been cheated in some way.

Ned took the pea and placed it under the middle shell then proceeded to shuffle them round and round, left to right, centre to side and back. The shells even went to the edge of the table in a furious figure of eight. Tyus and Seren kept their eyes peeled on the shell until it stopped. Ned pulled back his hands and folded his arms.

'Now my little ones, where is the rascal pea?'

Tyus was sure it was under the walnut on the right.

'I'm thinking the right,' he whispered to Seren and Joe.
"I think so too,' said Seren.

'I never took my eyes off it,' Joe agreed.

With his heart in his mouth, Tyus pointed to the shell on the right.

'Don't change your mind,' teased Ned.

Tyus shook his head. Ned upturned the shell. There was nothing in it. No pea.

'Bad luck, lad' chuckled Ned. 'I win, them's the rules. Hand over the dog and the crocodile.'

'Oh no,' sighed Seren.

One of the men dragged Rufus by his lead to their side of the tavern. Ned pocketed the key ring, trusting Captain Ranworth's opinion that it was valuable. He kept it close.

'Now get those mites out of here. They shouldn't be in a tavern at their age.' Ned growled.

'Wait!' said Captain Ranworth. 'Let's see what is under the other two shells.'

'Are you doubting me?' Ned asked turning pale.

'Just making sure the rules have been followed, as an independent observer.'

Ned nodded slowly. 'Of course, Captain, sir.'

There was a hush in the room. Ned upturned the middle shell – it was empty. Then, not waiting until the final shell was revealed, Will lost his patience.

'I knew it,' Will called out. 'He has to be cheating us. That's why I lost so many times.'

Everyone turned to look at the hapless Will but his outburst had given Ned enough time to slip the pea back under the last shell while everyone was distracted. Ned removed the remaining shell and there lay the pea, sitting sweetly, unaware of the trouble it was causing.

'There be it! Now I'll have your apology, Will Lowland.' Ned grinned. "Are you satisfied Captain Ranworth?'

Ranworth knew there was no more to be said. He tipped his hat and made to leave the tavern. He reached the door and breathed in the clear air. The children followed.

'I thought you would help us,' Seren said boldly as she passed him by. He stopped surprised by her forthrightness.

'She mean no harm, Captain,' interrupted Joe wiping a tear.

Captain Chad Ranworth surveyed the group. A strange trio, he thought. The boy, carrying unusual objects even he, as a ship's captain, had not seen on his voyages to Spain, Italy and the West Indies. He recognized the hardworking dairy hand from Gill Moss, who was constantly with the talented hound that many a folk would want to own, and the third, this outspoken maid. He would keep a watch on these children.

'Young lady, I am a gentleman, true to my word. There was no proof of wrongdoing. Maybe Farmer Langley should keep away from the tavern and making bets.' He nodded to Joe. 'I'm sorry,

Joe, I know you and your dog, Rufus, were inseparable.'

'How can we get him back?' pressed Seren.

Captain Ranworth smiled at her.

'You are a determined lass aren't you? Look, if you ever hear or see Rufus being mistreated or used in poaching, let me know and I'll see what I can do. There are laws about those crimes but I would need proof and then, he may be returned to you. Come to my home at Sparrow Hall with the evidence any time.'

'Thank you Captain,' said Joe, 'we will stay alert.'

'We wouldn't want any harm coming to Rufus – he's very special to us,' added Tyus.

The Captain buttoned up his coat, as the air was turning chilly. 'I can see that. You gave up a treasure to try to win him back. What was it made from?'

Tyus bit his lip. He knew he couldn't reveal they were from the future. The Captain continued.

'I've seen real crocodile skin and it wasn't that. I know real gold and it was far from being gold and I've held black onyx in my hand and I don't believe it was that either. I would be intrigued to know what is was and where it came from.'

'But you told Ned it was valuable – that's why he let us bet. You gave us a chance even though you knew it was fake,' Tyus said.

'They deserve to be deceived sometimes and I wanted you to find the pea and win back Rufus.'

'Then thank you for trying,' piped up Seren.

'No matter,' the Captain murmured. 'But if you want to tell me of your travels, you can trust me. I've sailed around the globe and seen things you wouldn't believe: volcanoes spewing out ash, birds that fly backwards, long legged birds that can't fly and birds whose legs bend backwards. I've seen people with rings high up their necks who live in remote villages but I've never seen anything like the object you took from your pocket.'

Tyus and Seren stood wide-eyed and unsure of how to answer. They would have to be careful. What would happen if they told him of their time tunnel? People might think they were ghosts like Joe or perhaps witches. Tyus had learnt in school about people accused of being a witch, for all sorts of reasons, many untrue, but mostly because they were different. It didn't end well. Luckily, Joe stepped in with a barrage of questions.

'Captain Ranworth, my greatest wish is to sail around the world. How do I learn to sail? What could I do to be part of a crew? Did you really see a bird fly backwards? Are dogs allowed on ships? When are you sailing again? Where are you going next time?'

The Captain laughed heartily.

'Now young Joe, enough questions! I thought you were destined to be a dairyman and live on the land. I've noticed you are a good worker. But now I can see a wanderlust for adventure and the high seas that I once had at your age.'

'I am a good worker and quick learner, Captain, and I can read and write.' Joe added hopefully.

'I like your curiosity.' Captain Ranworth studied Joe's earnest face. 'I am seeking new investment from Lord Molyneux and the Botanical society for my next voyage. My interest is to find and study new plants and animals, like Captain Cook's great, scientific voyages to the South Seas. So if you see any poaching on his lordship's land, tell me. I will inform the Earl, he may look favourably on my voyage and you might recover your dog.'

He smiled at the idea that he was making a plan with the young farmhand and two unusual children.

'Then I will have a new voyage where there may be room for an apprentice and a watchdog.'

Joe was astonished.

'Do you mean it, Captain?'

'You have my word as a gentleman,' the Captain replied. 'Now, I must be going. Good luck.'

He turned directly to Tyus and Seren and said something that made them both shiver.

'Good luck to all of you, for I fear you children are not from these parts and are unaware of the dangers here. Take extra care fellow travellers.'

3 MAB AND THE FIR TREES

SOLVE THE RIDDLE & SEEK THIS
**I'm somewhere between sky and ground, yet always moving away. What am I? **

'We're sorry about Rufus, Joe. We tried to help.' Tyus said.

Joe kicked a pebble along the gravelly road back to the farm. They had been walking slowly, each one of them lost in thought.

'It's fine, Tyus,' said Joe with a cheeky grin. 'You did your best. Rufus is clever. He will be well but you lost your jewel to Ned. I'm sorry you lost something so valuable.'

'It's not all bad,' Seren chimed in, 'we know where Rufus is and we can watch him. Captain Ranworth will help us when we get the evidence they are poaching.'

Joe leaned over the Stone Bridge and dropped three pebbles into the stream below.

'Look at the Alt stream, it never stops, it's bubbling along on its way to the sea. We're like the puny pebbles – too small to make any difference. The stream washes over them.'

Seren laughed. 'That's because you picked up three tiny pebbles.'

She jumped up on one of the larger boulders. 'Say we found three huge stones and we helped each other carry them into the stream. Would that make a difference?'

She jumped from the rock. 'Yes! It would change the flow of the water because we worked together.'

Now Joe laughed. 'You're a clever one, Miss Seren.'

'What she means Joe is that the three of us will work together to rescue Rufus and if the Captain helps too, anything can happen.'

This cheered Joe up and he ran the rest of the route to the farm leaping over the park stile at the entrance shouting, 'I've got chores first then we'll see.'

Joe's chores consisted of attaching the cart in the barn to a foal he called Lorenzo and loading the wagon with milk churns.

'I have to deliver milk to Stand House, way past the Fir Tree wood. There's an orchard there and we'll exchange the milk for apples. We'll fill the cart to the brim with apples on the journey back. Farmer Langley sells them at the market with his cheese each Quarter day.'

He patted the frisky foal on the neck. 'Lorenzo here could find his own way we've made the ride so often but I'm thinking, what if we took the shorter path through the fir trees instead of the road round the edge of the forest? It's narrower and we would have to watch for tree roots tripping the cart but we've done it before.'

'Whatever you say, Joe.' said Tyus. 'It will give us more time to make a plan.'

Joe took the reins and shuffled Lorenzo forward. 'Climb aboard my new friends, we're off to Stand House orchard and chicken farm!'

The three friends sat together on the driver's bench and rattled along the road watching Lorenzo's tail flip from side to side. They took the route north of the farm and soon reached the tall pines and evergreens of fir tree wood. A well-worn wide avenue circled the wood but they took a small turn along a less travelled path into the greenery of the forest. Joe picked up the speed of the cart with a skillful twist of his wrist and a shout out to Lorenzo. They jostled at a steady pace along the winding path bouncing out of their seat whenever a large root jolted the wheels of the cart.

'This is fun,' said Seren as they clattered along. She breathed in the cool forest air and watched the branches on the trees shake with the rhythm of the cart. The big wooden wheels crunched over pine needles and early autumn leaf fall.

'Can I take the reins, Joe?' asked Tyus. 'I'd love to try. Is it hard?'

Joe chortled. 'Nay, Tyus, here you are.'

He slipped the leather reins over Tyus's hands. 'Just keep it steady.'

Tyus felt the pull of the reins as Lorenzo quickened his beat. He was instantly aware of the novice driver and wanted to test how fast he could go. He whinnied and trotted over the uneven ground, skipping lightly over the long roots that appeared across his path occasionally. They were deep in the wood now and the sound of the wind in the spokes of the wheels whistled from tree to tree.

'Show me how to go faster,' Tyus asked, feeling more confident.

Joe explained how to hold the reins, the wheels clicked faster. The milk churns rattled with a metallic chime as they knocked into each other. Lorenzo sensed some sport and was ready to gallop when there was another sound, high pitched and shrill. Seren heard it first.

'Shh, you two, slow down.'

The boys ignored her and laughed loudly as Lorenzo took off at speed. Seren worried that the milk would be turned into butter or fall off the cart.

'Joe, please stop,' she cried, 'I heard something.'

The cart shook from side to side. The wind hit the boys' faces with a thrilling freshness. Tyus imagined he was driving a chariot on a racetrack and he was about to win.

'There it goes again!' Seren insisted. 'It sounds like a young sheep bleating and it's getting louder.'

'It's only the wind, it's nothing,' Tyus dismissed her worries and continued with his daydreaming. Now he was flying across the sky like Apollo.

She grabbed hold of the seat as they approached a narrow brook with a rickety bridge. They hurled uncontrollably towards the passing, picking up speed. The bleating became louder in Seren's ears. At this pace there was a danger they would end up in the ditch at the side of the bridge.

'Slow down Ty, I don't like it!'

Without warning, Seren placed her hands over the boys' eyes so they couldn't see where they were going. It was a drastic move but she had to try it. Being suddenly deprived of sight, Tyus and Joe panicked. Instinctively, they pushed her hand away but Tyus let go of the reins entirely. Would the cart buckle and crash? They held on tightly swerving through the hedges and trees. Joe instantly knew what to do. He grasped the reins and pulled Lorenzo up to a grinding halt just before the bridge.

'What did you do that for Seren?' Tyus asked crossly.

Seren jumped out of the cart, her face pink and her forehead wrinkled.

'I wanted you to stop.'

'But that was reckless and dangerous,' Tyus called after her.

She swept a tendril of her golden hair from her eyes. 'I'm sorry. I thought I heard a cry for help. Someone's in trouble.'

Joe caught his breath and patted down Lorenzo's neck.

'People hear many strange sounds in the woods. It can make you do things you shouldn't.'

Seren realised the boys were puzzled by her behaviour.

'Can we be quiet for a moment and listen so I know I didn't imagine it?'

Tyus climbed down from the driver's seat and stood next to her. She had that serious look on her face she got when she sensed something.

'We'll listen,' said Tyus nodding over at Joe.

The woods were quiet. There was no birdsong just a gentle breeze through the trees. Tyus tipped his head back as if he could hear something in the sky or way up in the tallest branches of the fir trees. After a minute, Joe became restless. He shifted his feet and stretched out an arm but said nothing. Seren gestured to them to be still for one more minute with her finger. She heard the tiny cry once more and looked for confirmation from the boys. This time they had heard it too. Still standing still, they searched the area with their eyes. It was close, sounding not like a lamb that had lost its way in the forest but a voice – a person.

'Help me!' the shrill tones said clearer now.

'Where are you?' Seren asked.

They followed the voice along the ditch where a branch had fallen.

'Help me!' it begged again, 'I'm here, by the branch.'

'This is trickery,' said Joe, 'there's nothing here. Let's go.' He stepped back towards the cart but it called again.

'I'm trapped under the log.'

Seren and Tyus tiptoed forward scrutinizing the branch. No one seemed to be trapped under it.

'Come away,' called Joe, 'it's the spirits of the forest making mischief.'

'Tell me if I am close,' Seren said undaunted.

She began tapping the log starting at the end and working her way to the middle. The person screamed in a voice that made everyone's heart jump.

'I'm here!'

The children pushed the log together rolling it up on to the bank. Then they saw the tiny owner of the voice, a woman about the size of a pebble. She wriggled from the mud and suddenly flew above their heads wobbling like a sleepy firefly, for this diminutive creature had butterfly wings twice the size of her. She shook off the dirt from her delicate wings and brushed down her grasshopper green hair and gossamer gown. She hovered unsteadily above their heads, gazing into their astonished faces with her turquoise eyes before landing with a bump on Joe's shoulders. Seren noticed one of her wings was damaged.

'Help! Get it off me,' yelled Joe. 'Take it away! It be a sprite. There be mischief here.'

'Don't move, you'll hurt her,' said Seren gently lifting her off his shoulders. She cupped the creature in her hand.

'She's beautiful.' Seren placed her onto the soft grass. 'Are you all right? Can we help you?'

'Don't speak to it!' screeched Joe.

The fairy creature attempted to move again but after a few tries realised it was no good and sat forlornly on the grass.

'What is whiter than snow and softer than silk?' she cried out so shrilly Joe almost fell from the cart.

'Answer the riddle!' the fairy demanded urgently.

Seren frowned. 'Whiter than snow – a cloud maybe?'

The fairy shivered and her wing shriveled up.

'Or wool on a sheep,' Tyus guessed.

She shivered again and the wing started to break up. If they guessed wrongly next time, the wing might fall off entirely. Tyus and Seren nervously looked at Joe.

'I knows it,' said Joe, 'it's me she's on about.'

He jumped down from the cart and knelt down where the tiny woman sat cross-legged on the grass.

'I knows the answer fairy, and then we go safely. Do you agree?'

She looked at him hopefully but said nothing. Joe began.

'Whiter than snow and softer than silk, a dairyman knows the answer is milk.'

Immediately, her wing filled out to its full size and began healing itself.

'It's working. Well done Joe,' cried Seren.

The fairy flew into the air once more, this time the wings fluttered quicker and stronger. She darted from one to the other before hovering in front of them.

'Thank you,' she spoke kindly. 'Solving the riddle healed my wings. I have been trapped under the branch for many days. I was gathering lemon balm and mustard garlic for my work. People don't come through the forest often and they are in such a hurry they would never hear my cries, but you did. There is a gleaming about you that others don't possess. Perhaps that is why you could hear.'

She smiled at Seren then turned to Joe.

'You were ready to solve my riddle even though you were afraid of forest spirits.
She flew over to Tyus spinning and testing her repaired wing.

'And you did not fear me although I am different from you and not from your world. You raised the branch.'

She trembled in mid air, her dress shimmering with the movement.

'Now, I must reward you for that is the fairy way.'

'A fairy!' Seren gasped as the tiny lady floated up between the trees.

'My cottage is here.'

A sign read 'Thimble Hall' high up in the tree. The fairy opened a tiny door hidden in the trunk and returned with a small tube shaped bottle containing clear liquid. She presented the phial to Seren.

'I am Mab, Queen of the night,
Folk believe I'm a naughty sprite,
You were kind, though you were afraid,
So I will give you a potion of shade,
Over hill, over dale,
Over park, over vale,
Through bush, through briar,
Make men's dreams your desire.'

'We don't want any reward,' said Joe firmly but it was too late. Seren held the bottle in her hand.

'What does it do?' questioned Tyus.

'Did you not understand?' Mab spun round Tyus's head. 'Droplets of the potion will make anyone dream what you want them to dream. It is a sleep potion.'

'Take nothing from her,' Joe climbed aboard the cart but Mab laughed. She was used to humans fearing her. She continued her spell.

'Mab can make a man dream
he is a swan,
a lady dream of love
or a boy run
with a fiery dragon
or a maiden fair
ride a unicorn
high into the air.
Some think I make mischief for I deceive,
But I give folk what they need to believe.'

'Take care of the potion. You will need it before you return home. Farewell friends,' Mab shrilled as she twirled upwards into the trees and disappeared from sight leaving the children speech-less.

Stand House came into view as the children reached the edge of the dark woodland and emerged from the emerald gloom of the fir trees. It was a square stone building surrounded by white fences and chicken sheds. The farmer heard the rickety sound of the wheels and set his angry jaw firm. He stood with his hands on his hips and did not return Joe's usual grin, wider than usual now he had escaped his encounter with Mab.

'Good afternoon Farmer Leamington, milk from Gill Moss dairy as ordered.'

'You are late Joseph Kirkby. What do you mean by coming through the fir wood and with strangers? There's enough upset going about without you changing your delivery route.' The farmer eyed Tyus and Seren suspiciously.

'Sorry sir, I had an extra chore for Farmer Langley so the forest road was quicker but milk is here. These be new friends of mine.'

Tyus and Seren smiled angelically but Farmer Leamington never flinched.

'And where be your dog that never leaves your side?'

Joe's face fell. He'd been having an adventure in the woods and forgotten about Rufus. Now he felt ashamed he hadn't thought of him, however briefly.

'He, he's gone.' Joe stuttered.

Farmer Leamington shouted angrily. 'I know he's gone because he's been here worrying my chickens! They nearly got out.'

'But I left him with Ned Lewis and his men at the Dog and Gun, on Langley's orders,' Joe added quickly.

The farmer stamped over to the gate and checked the locks.

'Now I see it. It was definitely your golden haired hound. They are training him to hunt chickens and geese. He was here sniffing the coops and releasing the locks. Those poachers would have taken my whole stock too but just at the final minute, your dog barked wildly, must have been when the apple pile suddenly gave way. Maybe the noise startled him, the rumbling hill slide sound they make. Anyways, he barked so much the chickens fled and I came out from my house with my musket. If Ned and his men were there, they must have escaped and your dog ran off with them.'

'Rufus wouldn't hurt your chickens,' Joe protested. 'He meant no harm, sir.'

'I recognized him all right with his sandy fur and if I see him again, I'll blast him out of the way. Once a dog has gone bad, there's no getting him back.' Farmer Leamington decided. 'Now, let's be unloading these milk churns.'

4 CRAVEN WOOD

FIND THE HIDDEN WORD
Deer were frightened by the noise.

T he evening was closing in. In a moment, the pale, dying embers of the sun would be gone. The three friends crouched beneath two, thick tree trunks. Joe had provided them with woollen blankets and food from the farmhouse. Eating bread and cheese, wrapped up warmly, had never felt so cosy.

'We could be in for a long night,' mumbled Joe between bites. 'Luckily we managed to sleep earlier after my chores. The poachers might come out tonight or not. They might go poaching in another wood.'

Seren sighed. 'You know the area, Joe, I trust you. I bet you've made the right guess. Your plan to see if Rufus is being used by Ned for poaching is our only hope.'

Joe's smile stretched from ear to ear. He puffed out his chest.

'Well there's Dam Wood yonder or even Mull Wood – but the gamekeeper lives there. He works for the Earl to keep poachers away. The Kennels are nearby too, they could disturb the dogs, so I believe they'll try here – Craven Wood. It be named after the Earl's wife's family and it's full of rabbits.'

'It's worth a try,' said Tyus. 'If Ned and the poachers come out tonight, we can tell Captain Ranworth and claim Rufus back.'

'We might need more proof. There will be three hunting outings. First, they let Rufus at the chickens like at Stand Lodge...' Joe began.

'Yes, but he barked and disturbed Farmer Leamington. Rufus may have barked on purpose to let the chickens get away.' Seren interrupted.

Tyus and Joe laughed. It would be a crafty notion worthy of Rufus.

'True, Miss Seren,' said Joe. His eyes looked into the distance for a moment. 'I'm sorry my dog isn't by my side right now.'

'Come on,' cajoled Tyus, 'first the chickens...'

'Oh aye, ' said Joe, ' first chickens. Then, I think it will be rabbits and Craven Wood is best for rabbits. There's plenty of other wildlife here too, especially birds. I've seen nuthatch, jackdaw, collared dove even woodpecker and by the ponds, mallards and moorhens. It's teeming with field mice and rabbits and it's a cloudy night – the moon is hid.'

Joe licked his finger and held it up to the wind. He turned his body about in right angles, testing the direction like a human compass.

'Whatever happens, we sit downwind from the poachers so their dogs can't smell us. We'll watch them and get evidence. Meanwhile, let's gather bracken.'

Following Joe's lead, Tyus and Seren gathered the bracken and piled it up against a rock between the trees. They soon made a shelter where they could stay hidden from anyone passing by.

'We should be safe here,' said Joe.

They draped the blankets on their shoulders like cloaks and sat down to wait. They began the stake out in earnest.

'Rufus will scent us I'm sure,' mused Tyus. 'I hope he doesn't give us away. If he alerts Ned, we'll be found.'

'Rufus wouldn't do that,' Seren whispered, 'even after all this time, he still remembers us.'

'He's the loyalist dog I ever met,' said Joe. 'I hope he knows we are trying to bring him back.'

They huddled quietly, listening to the last calls of chiff chaff and willow warbler before the sun set completely and the sky turned charcoal grey.

'I can't believe I saw a fairy!' Seren gasped at the memory of Mab.

'Please, I begged you not to speak of her,' Joe quivered. 'We were lucky to escape with our lives. Fairy spirits and human kind do not speak.'

'She was a kind fairy,' said Tyus, 'at least to us. We helped her and she said we might need the potion she gave us.'

Nervously Joe broke a twig he had been holding in his hands.

'I'm having nothing more to say but I swear to you I'll never take a short cut through Fir Tree Wood again.' He gathered his makeshift cloak tighter round his chest.

Slowly shapes appeared coming through the wood. Men in dark clothes, hooded, with only their faces peeping through, came stealthily through the foliage. They had smeared their cheeks with dirt from the forest floor and were carrying empty sacks thrown over their shoulders. Others carried nets and snares.

'It's them,' breathed Seren, 'and look there's Rufus!'

They watched as the men approached the clearing. Rufus led the way followed by several other dogs, which waited while Rufus sniffed out the rabbits' burrows before alerting their owners with a soft whine. The men set their traps where Rufus had indicated and moved on deeper into the wood.

'Come along, Marie,' called Ned to one of the poachers at the back.

A girl! Tyus thought.

'I don't know why I promised your mother I would take you poaching Marie, keep up!'

The girl forced herself to the front of the group. She was wearing a man's hat and coat.

'I can run and jump as well as any and be faster than most too,' she said looking at Will from the tavern, who was also with the group. Marie elbowed past him digging him in his side with the staff she was carrying.

'Aye, and you'll be fined by the same magistrate if you are caught,' Will called out trying to hide his pain. 'Do you have two shillings and sixpence or will you have to go to gaol?'

'Ease off, young Will, she'll have her uses collecting the spoil. I doubt they'll send the young lass to gaol like us lads. Some say us poachers are stealing but it is only sport I attest,' said Ned. 'Trying to outwit a pheasant say and a gamekeeper, then take it home to make a pot to feed the family – how is that a crime? It's the landowners' fault fencing off the land as private property.'

'So, how many rabbits are we bagging tonight, uncle?' Marie coaxed.

'With this dog, I expect we'll fill a hundred pots and hundred more we'll sell on to Manchester or Liverpool,' he laughed. 'I have a big family,' he lied.

The gang trampled further, laying more nets as Rufus led them away from the den where the children were listening. Tyus slipped on the moss snapping a twig under his weight. In the distance, he saw Rufus's ears stand up but it was Will who frowned and turned his head to where they were. He started walking towards them slowly, staring at the bracken still rubbing his side. He was sure he could feel a bruise coming. The children held their breath; frozen with fear they were about to be discovered. They heard his boots crunch on the early fallen leaves he was so close. Their muscles tensed ready to flee when Marie came running back to Will.

'Will, my uncle Ned said I had to fetch you in case you got lost.' She tapped him on the arm. 'I see you've already taken the wrong path, blunderbuss!'

Will did not like to be teased. He scowled at her.

'I'm not lost. I was investigating. I thought I heard…'

But Marie was running back to the gang giggling so Will followed her, sprinting to catch her up and overtake her if he could.

'That was close,' said Tyus, 'these men are serious poachers. I'm sure the Captain would want to know.'

Seren had a more urgent question.

'Poor Rufus! What will happen if they are caught?'

'Forest law is strict,' said Joe. 'If the gamekeeper finds them, he could seize their muskets and dogs, so likely Rufus would be taken by the crown.'

'This is bad; we have to go to Sparrow Hall to tell Captain Ranworth to stop it. You never said anything about muskets. They weren't carrying any tonight as far as I could see?' Tyus questioned.

Joe kicked the bracken with his feet and jumped up.

'That was the third thing I was going to say. One: the chickens with dogs. Two: the rabbits with nets. Three: deer with muskets. I think the next night they hunt, it will be for deer and deer are the property of the king under protection of the Earl. If they are caught, we'll never see Rufus again.'

Towards dawn, a sullen light crept into the sky. The children watched from a safe distance as Ned and his poaching gang loaded up their wagons with the bulging sacks from the night's hunting. Mist was hanging low across the meadow as they bid each other a good morning. One by one they drifted off to their homes, a steady stare of defiance on their faces in place, if their illegal actions were to be challenged by anyone who would stop them on their way. The rabbits would be sold for a pretty penny and eventually each would get his share.

Will and Marie were continuing to spar and argue. She pushed him into the wagon and laughed as he rubbed his hip, which had made contact with the wheel with a sick thud. Ned made no attempt to calm things. Marie's voice cut through the morning mist.

'Have you had time to ponder my plan, uncle? Is it not something daring?'

Ned scratched his back and bent his knees.

'I am thinking on it, Marie, but it is an impudent plan. You say there are important guests up at the Hall.'

'I know there are. I saw them with my own eyes. As maid-of-all-work I can roam the Hall quite freely. I saw them – Frenchmen dressed in finest silk and lace, highborn they are, maybe a count or a prince. They are visiting the Earl but Will thinks my plan a stupid idea.'

Will threw his hands up in the air.

'Doesn't matter what I think. Marie's the cunning one. She's working the Hall by day and poaching at night. Coming up with plans to kidnap French princes.'

Tyus and Joe gulped. 'Did you hear that?' said Joe.

'Shh!' said Seren, 'keep listening.'

'It is a good plan,' Ned decided. 'If we take a deer or two when we go hunting tonight, we might make good money but it is dangerous. If we are caught it will be prison for sure but if we kidnap a Frenchman, the Earl will pay handsomely to keep it quiet and we will be richer than we ever imagined.'

'Most likely, one of them will be alone on Sunday for prayers. I heard them talking,' Marie said. 'He's the one they call the Count of Artois.'

Marie and her uncle took the front seats on top of the wagon. The children could see Rufus asleep in the cart weary after the night's stalking. Will took his place at the back of the cart on a small ledge. His head was bent low staring at the floor with his feet brushing the ground. Ned flicked his wrist and the old horse heaved the cart along the road.

Tyus and Seren turned to Joe, their eyes wide with disbelief.

'Have we enough evidence for Captain Ranworth? We must stop the deer hunt or Rufus will be confiscated and what shall we do about the kidnapping plan?' Tyus asked.

Joe nodded slowly and raised his eyebrows. 'There is more than enough for the Captain but I think we should go straight to the Hall and tell the Earl himself.'

5 CROXTETH HALL

The early mist that had hovered over the fields thickened and followed them as the children made their way to one of the lodges on the Earl's estate. For centuries the lodges had stood on the corners of the parkland owned by the Earl and the Molyneux family. They were manned by lodge keepers who were challenged with keeping out curious passers by or villagers without an invitation. Anyone unknown to the Earl was unlikely to be allowed through the gates. It was going to be difficult for children to persuade the lodge keeper that they had vitally important information for the Earl.

'Have you ever seen the Earl, Joe?' Tyus asked.

'Not really,' replied Joe. 'Farmer Langley said he saw the old Earl once, walking by one of the ponds. The new Earl, his son, is always in a hurry. It's hard to get a glimpse of him. I saw his carriage charge past the Stone Bridge like a wild cat in the summer. William Philip Molyneux, 2nd Earl of Sefton is his full name. I've heard he is a sportsman.'

'Which sport?' Tyus was interested to know and wondered if football had been invented yet.

'He has a nickname. He's called Lord Dashalong because he has a mad fondness for racing the four white horses on his carriage. It doesn't matter to him if he's in the park or on the streets of London. But he's an expert I've heard tell.'

Tyus and Joe slapped their sides and began to 'gallop' through the thickening fog, imagining how fast four horses could carry them. Certainly faster than Lorenzo and that had been fun. Seren hurried after them before their shapes disappeared from sight.

'Whoa, horses!' she called into the void. It was eerie how quickly the fog had reduced visibility. For a second Seren felt alone in the fog, then she saw the boys had stopped.

A squat, single storey stone building loomed in the shadows. A flickering candle had been placed in the window and the forbidding, large silhouette of the lodge keeper could be seen moving inside.

'I'm worried the keeper will think our story unbelievable,' Seren said aloud into the mist.

Tyus pushed his hands into his pockets and turned up the collar on his jacket. He had been thinking the same thing and had a plan.

'If we can get to the Hall, someone will listen – especially if the guests are in danger. The hardest part will be persuading the gatekeeper to let us pass but the fog could help us. It's thicker here and we are small – smaller than the look out window.'

'And the fog makes everything quiet,' added Seren following his thread. 'It dulls sounds.'

'We could slip past easily. What do you say, Joe?' Tyus continued.

Joe nodded. 'I'll give it a try. I could loosen the gate and squeeze past. But if we are caught – get ready to run!'

Silently, they crept nearer the lodge window, keeping their

heads low. Under the veil of the fog, Joe unfastened the lock on the gate. Tyus and Seren slipped through but Joe lingered a moment too long before refastening the gate and it shut with a metallic clunk.

The lodge keeper rubbed his eyes and whiskers and ran to the lodge door to check.

'Who's there?' he bellowed into the grey pillow of fog but the children had melted into the mist and had begun the long walk down the driveway up to the Hall.

The Molyneuxs, who had built the hall, were an old French family come to England with William the Conqueror in 1066. Through making pacts and friendships with important people, they gained more wealth and lands. For centuries they supported the monarchs. They were given huge forests filled with deer and pheasant for the rich to hunt. Their beautiful and impressive home they called Croxteth Hall. It stood at the fringes of the ancient village of West Derby. The family became richer and built another wing in Queen Anne's reign and now it had two hundred rooms. Many horses were kept in the stables and paddock. The garden staff grew their own produce for the kitchen staff to prepare meals. The new Earl, William, (Lord Dashalong) had married Maria Craven from another wealthy family and they were making Croxteth Hall their family home.

The Earl was also a lover of hunting, a gambler and friend to the King's son, Prince George. His coat of arms was a shield with a cross Moline which also adorned the front of his house. One theory says it was called 'moline' because the ends of the cross, split and curved into two branches, like found in a mill. Moline was Old French for mill. The family may also hail from the town of Moulin.

The chilly, foggy mist draped itself round the tall oaks and sycamores causing droplets of water to fall on the children's shoulders as they trod along the driveway. A feeble light appeared ahead of them, then two. There was muffled shouting and rattling.

'Are we near the Hall, Joe? What are those lights?' Tyus asked.

'We must be nearing it now,' said Joe as the rattling noises increased and more lights appeared.

'They're coming this way,' said Seren, 'what shall we do?'

Instinctively, Tyus pulled them down into the undergrowth by the side of the path. Men carrying fiery torches ran by, lining both sides of the road. They waved the flames high above their heads and were shouting to each other.

'They're lighting the way for someone,' guessed Tyus correctly, for from nowhere, careering between the torchlights came a fine coach pulled by four, ghostly, white horses. The horses soon outran the torchbearers, being driven hard by an unseen coachman and rattled on blindly into the mist. It pounded past the children. Voices, laughing and cajoling the driver to drive with more abandon, emerged from the carriage as it sped by out of sight. The torchbearers retraced their steps back to the hall.

'That was the Earl's coach, we've missed him,' said Joe disappointedly.

'I hope that coachman can see in the dark,' joined in Tyus. 'They were going too fast to stop. Lucky we stepped aside.'

'Now who are we going to give our information to?' Seren wondered gloomily.

Another torchlight flickered from out of nowhere.

'What information?'

A girl, with black hair to her waist, slightly older than Tyus, stood in front of them. She wore a long blue dress covered in ribbons and a full cloak tied with a bow. She waved the torch before her.

'Where did you spring from?' Tyus asked startled.

'*You* do not ask questions. It is more interesting for me to know why you are trespassing, no? She replied in a French accent.

'Oh, are you French?' said Seren unalarmed, 'Are you with the French people up at the hall?'

She thrust the torch in Seren's face and then waved it in front of the boys' faces.

'Urchins!' she cried.

Joe stood in front of Seren protecting her from the flame.

'I may be an urchin, but my friends are high born,' he smiled at Seren, 'but we do have an important message for the Earl that concerns his guests.'

The girl moved her torch to illuminate their clothes and shoes then up to their rosy faces again. Urchins did not wear clothes like this.

'Then you must tell me. I have authority. My name is Therese Baland, daughter of Chef Baland, master charcutier to Le Comte d' Artois. Again, what is the information?'

'We can only give the information to the Earl or the Count,' repeated Joe.

'Then you are too late, monsieur. As you see, the Comte has gone out to lunch in his carriage for the feast day and the Earl is not expected back from Liverpool until tonight.'

'Then tell us where they have gone,' Tyus spoke up, 'lives may depend upon it.'

'Or would you take us there?' said Seren.

The girl raised her eyebrows, taken aback by their lack of deference. She studied Seren's glittery top and unusual clothing. These children were not peasants and they had something in their bearing even the boy urchin.

'Very well, I will lead the way. They are feasting at Monks Down abbey but I warn you, if you are lying, they will be angry.'

6 MONKS DOWN

FIND TWO WORDS IN THIS ACROSTIC

***

Giles the hermit
Lived on mountain high
Among the deer that he
Loved and cared for till the tomb.
Prayers bring miracles so,
Now at feasts and fairs be merry.
***

A s they walked towards the lodge led by Therese with her torch, the fog began to lift. The weak, early sun gave way to his stronger noontime brother and burnt back the mist with his heat. Therese stood before the gates until the lodge keeper unlocked them and without thanks, marched silently by, her three followers trotting like ducklings behind mother duck.

She glanced back at her tired and dirty entourage and scoffed something under her breath, unaware that they had been awake most of the night in the forest. She did notice their determined jaws and steely eyed stares and wondered what valuable piece of information they held.

Her father, the Great Chef, who travelled with the Count to prepare his meals, had left before dawn to begin preparations for the special feast at Monks Down, an old abbey no longer in use. Present would be Le Comte d'Artois and his attendants - Baron de

Rolles and the Duc de Berri. The Earl's business in the city meant he was unable to join his guests for the lunch.

'You are risking the wrath of the Comte if you lie. He does not like festivities interrupted by peasants,' she goaded but with a wry smile as her new companions were beginning to amuse her.

Seren was bubbling with annoyance but Tyus tapped her gently on the arm and whispered, 'Calm.'

Tyus drew up alongside Therese and ignoring her comment said, 'Are you going to the feast?'

She shrugged. 'I am merely helping my father to prepare the food, assisting with last minute things, dressing the dishes with sweetmeats and such.'

'It sounds important,' gushed Tyus trying to be charming. She was so serious but very pretty for a girl, he thought.

'It is,' Therese smiled reluctantly. This peasant seems refined she thought, softening.

Seren rolled her eyes at Joe and giggled. She could tell her brother was using flattery but it was still odd to hear him. They past a familiar green grove with almond trees and came to a narrow stream trickling over stepping-stones.
'We cross here by the Abbot's ford,' said Therese. 'The monastery is not far now.'

'I thought it is forbidden to be a priest or a monk?' asked Tyus.

Therese shot him an angry look. 'It is difficult,' she explained. 'Some monks have been allowed to return to care for the buildings, which have been falling into ruin. If they keep out of the way of the authorities, they are left alone. It is small steps you say? But we are friends, no? You will not betray, I think.'

'We are friends,' said Tyus strongly. 'We are hoping to prevent trouble and help Joe get his dog back.'

For the first time, Therese looked concerned. Tyus noticed the slight change in her face.

'Joe's dog, Rufus, has become part of a poaching gang. Rufus is a good dog, an excellent hunter but he has been working on a farm and is Joe's best friend. The information we have, we hope, will mean Rufus will be taken from the poachers and returned to Joe.'

'Poaching is against the law,' said Therese. 'It is possible if he is caught with the poachers he will be destroyed.'

'Yes, but Rufus doesn't really belong to them. The farmer lost a bet. We must help him escape.'

'You and the girl?' she started to say.

'My sister, Seren,' said Tyus. 'My name is Tyus. This is Joe, our friend.' Therese nodded for him to continue.

'We know Rufus from long ago. He is a special hound, very brave and loyal.'

They reached the monastery gates. The red-bricked outhouses had fallen into ruin but a long narrow building lay at the end of the path, the old refectory or dining room. It was in good repair with whitewashed walls and large windows. The Earl's coach, that had flown passed them on the Hall driveway, was there and empty of its passengers. The fog had lifted and the sun was warm on their backs. Therese extinguished the last embers of the torch. She called out.

'Par ici! Over here!'

A hooded figure saw them lingering by the gates. He yawned as he reached for the keys he kept on a belt on his waist. Two yapping spaniels sprang to their feet and wagged their tails in welcome when they heard Therese. They ran ahead of the man to the gates.

'Password?' The man grumbled.

'Happy St Giles's day, Brother Christopher,' she said.

The man opened the gates and the dogs immediately demanded Therese's attention. She stroked their necks and smiled at Tyus.

'You are not the only ones to enjoy the company of dogs. These rascals belong to my father but they love me just as much. Come, we will go to the kitchens first.'

The word 'kitchen' released a cauldron of smells into the air that they had not noticed till then. Potatoes, carrots, onions, herbs, ham and chicken smells wafted from the kitchen door at the end of the building, which was open. Joe felt his stomach grumble aloud. Tyus and Seren were hungry too.

Therese led them past the refectory. Through the windows they could see long tables laid out for a feast and set with goblets and plates. A fire burnt brightly at the top of the room. Men were eating and drinking and making merry, their faces pink with the warmth and the wine. The festivities had begun.

'This way,' insisted Therese. They reached the kitchen. Outside the coach and horses waited patiently until they were needed again. The horses were enjoying a feed, their heads buried deep in their nosebags. The coachmen sat together nearby with tankards of mead and plates of steaming food on their laps. They were laughing and sharing jokes.

A man with a red face, wearing a crisp, white jacket stood on the threshold looking worried.

'Therese, why are you late? Where have you been?' he fussed.

'Father,' Therese hugged him. 'I'm fine. We decided I was not needed until the desserts, remember?'

The man's face relaxed. 'Of course, bien sur. I was concerned about the fog. Who are these people with you?'

Therese studied her tired trio of followers. 'They walked with me from the Hall. They carry news for the Comte but can they wash up here first?'

Her father nodded in agreement.

'I understand. Most certainly, you cannot meet the Comte d'Artois like that. Come in, clean up, have some lunch. It is the feast day after all! Happy St Giles's Day!'

Tyus, Seren and Joe were shown into a room where they could wash their hands and faces and wipe away the dirt from the forest. They returned to the kitchen where Chef Baland served them with some broth, crusty bread and a large slice of meat cut from a side of beef roasting by the fire. A plate of plump sausages sat in the centre of the table. Seren chuckled as Joe's fork speared the sizzling sausage and guided it into his mouth until the juice spurted out.

Therese slipped off her cloak and began to assist her father with the cakes. Several large desserts awaited Therese's skills. She took up a piping bag and decorated each one with cream or edible flowers turning plain cakes into astounding works of art.

'Therese had explained to me your mission,' the Chef began. 'It would be best if you wait until the lunch feast is over and the gentlemen are engaged in the games. The Comte will be in a more agreeable mood to listen than if you disturb his meal.'

All agreed and finished their meals with a sample of one of the cakes.

'I can see how the Count wouldn't want to be disturbed if he's having food like this,' guzzled Joe. 'This is food for a king!'

Therese sat next to Tyus at the end of the bench. He scrunched up to make more room for her.

'You're very clever, Therese,' he said. 'These cakes are amazing.'

'Merci Tyus,' she said his name slowly, ' I hope they are fit for a king. The Comte d'Artois is the highest royalty in France.'

'I've heard France doesn't have a king anymore,' blurted Joe between crumbs. 'The people were starving and imprisoned him.' He devoured another mouthful of cake.

'You cannot stop being a king even if your country decides they don't want one,' retorted Therese. 'Oui, Yes, France has had a revolution and removed King Louis XVI, who was the Comte's brother, and his wife Marie Antoinette but now the Comte could become king in the future. He is our royal family. That is how it is.'

'Oh, I've heard about that,' said Tyus vaguely remembering some history lesson. 'Weren't the king and queen guillotined?'

'Heads removed!' cut in Joe unthinking. He bit off the top of whipped cream cake and wiped a blob of cream from his nose.

Therese stood up and blessed herself.

'It was a few years ago, in 1793. That is why the Comte and his family had to leave France. Your King George has been kind and given us shelter and safety here.'

'Then our information is important,' said Seren. 'Please may we tell the Count what we know?'

'Very well,' said the chef, 'follow me. We shall see if it can be accommodated. You are lucky it is the feast of St Giles of Nimes and everyone is in a joyful mood.'

The music from the refectory certainly sounded joyful. Chef Baland opened the door to violin, recorder and drum. The musicians sat in a corner away from the main tables. Every so often, the monks and their French guests would bang on the table with their fists in time to the beat. This was followed by peals of laughter and a toast.

The monks sat on long benches either side of the table. They wore simple tunics to their ankles that were hoisted up as they sat, to reveal thin hairy legs or rounded chubby calves. Their feet were bare in leather sandals. One was feeding a pet mouse under the table with crumbs. In the far corner, a parakeet on a rail squawked with excitement enjoying the din. Another monk sneezed several times and gulped a drink of water. His companion, red faced and warm, the taste of spicy meat in his mouth, wiped his brow with a large cloth.

At the end of the monks' table was another table laid across it to form a letter T shape. On this top table sat the guests of honour – the Abbot, the Count and his companions, feasting and making merry. Their colourful clothes were in stark contrast to the monks. They wore silk shirts decorated with lace and ruffles and elaborate waistcoats with silver thread.

The Count himself stood out in his frock coat and deep blue breeches trimmed with buttons and gold braid. The Duke of Berry and the Baron of Rolles were playing the Game of the Goatee or Jeu de la Barbichette, which was providing entertainment for the Count and the Abbot. The Count loved having fun and was known for inventing new games. He had a whole pleasure palace built in France for his games and entertainments.

The Duke and the Baron sat across from each other and looked at each other in the eye. The object of the game was to grab the other's chin. Whoever laughed first was the loser and his opponent could slap him – playfully! But it was getting out of hand as the Baron of Rolles seemed to be winning all the rounds and the Duke of Berry was not happy. His cheeks were burning with being slapped so much. As he was the Count's son, the Count was looking for a reason to halt the game without spoiling the fun. It was at that moment he caught sight of Chef Baland and the children.

'My friends, what have we here?' the Count gestured to the Chef to step inside.

Chef Baland bowed deeply.

'Forgive the intrusion, sir, but these children claim to have important and urgent information for you.'

The room fell silent as all eyes turned to the children. Therese pushed Tyus forward then stepped back quickly.

'Don't look at anyone,' she whispered, 'go to the Comte.'

Tyus walked slowly towards the high table. The Duke of Berry smiled; relieved his losing streak had come to an end.

'What is it, boy? Say your piece,' the Count demanded.

Tyus cleared his throat and bowed.

'Your lives are in danger. We overheard poachers plotting to kidnap you.'

The Count roared with laughter.

'Tres amusant. Very funny.' He took out a white lace handkerchief and waved it in the air. Everyone laughed.

'Poachers!' he continued, 'like I am like an animal they can snare! Little children, do you know who I am?'

Tyus, Seren and Joe nodded but he did not need them to answer. He took to the floor and paced about the room.

'The citizens of France have uprooted centuries of institutions – including the monarchy - because they say we spend too much while they are starving. But everyone knows the shortage was because of two decades of poor harvests. That was the true cause of the unrest amongst the people and the peasants.'

'Hear, hear!' said the Duke of Berry.

The Count turned to the Baron and winked.

'Someone had to pay taxes to fix it.'

The Baron took a sip of wine and saluted the Count. 'Not us, everyone else!'

'They guillotined my brother, his majesty Louis XVI and his beautiful wife and my friend, Marie Antoinette, you know. Yet despite that, I am here. I survive. Why?'

He looked round for an answer. The other guests smiled vacantly.

'Because I have been chosen of course – by God! I will return to France one day and be King.'

Everyone applauded.

'Poachers are not going to kidnap me. I fear them not!' he added.

'We might think differently if one of the poachers goes by the name of Napoleon Bonaparte – but I think not. Ha!' The Duke of Berry joked but no one laughed. Jesting about Napoleon wasn't funny. He was becoming too powerful in France.

'They be local men, no French amongst them,' clarified Joe.

'Then, thank you for the information, monsieur, but we are unafraid.' The Count reached for one of the cakes Therese had prepared. 'Now we will return to our feast!'

He flicked his hand and the Chef ushered the children to the door. Seren called out boldly.

'Please be careful, your majesty. We want no harm to come to you.'

'Mademoiselle, we are well guarded. We survived the revolution but your compassion for me is touching.' The Comte d'Artois beamed.

He took some gold coins from an embroidered bag on the table.

'My philosophy is to repair not demolish. Here is a guinea each for your trouble. Merci and Happy St Giles's Day to you!'

7 SEDGE MOOR

Ned Lewis had built his house at the edge of a wild, grassy field of sedge. The sedge grew tall and flowered in an unkempt way that somehow pleased him.

Rufus lapped up the remaining water from the bowl. At least he had been provided with a good meal after the long night of rabbit snaring. He remembered Joe had spoken softly in his ear when he handed him over to Ned. His voice had been calm and soothing. Rufus knew Joe would be back for him but in the meantime, he would have to stay with the poachers. He knew Tyus and Seren would not let him down. He had helped them find their father and protected them. They had shown courage and determination to rescue their Dad and he trusted they would aid Joe to rescue him.

He surveyed the cramped cottage where Ned had taken him and stretched his legs. Some of the poachers were finishing off a huge lunch of roasted rabbit and swilling down tankards of ale. Ned wiped the liquid from his lips with the back of his hand.

'A good haul last night, lads. We'll be dining on rabbit for a few days.' He tried to sound upbeat but the faces on his dining companions told a different story.

One grey whiskered man, known as Old Tom, was rubbing his thumb along a knot in the wood in the table before he spoke.

'Ned, rabbit will keep our families' bellies full for a while but we have too much because of that dog. Our contacts failed to show up in the fog now we have sacks of rabbit going bad and no money.'

Ned banged the table with his fist. 'No complaints! The dog sniffed out more rabbit holes than I've ever known. It's not his fault the fog came down and your buyers lost their way. He's a lucky dog. Remember, I won him in a bet.'

From the corner of his eye he noticed a young poacher, with brooding eyes named Matty, tapping his fingers on his chair.

'And what about the chickens up at Stand House? That went wrong with his barking,' Matty ventured, glaring at Rufus.

'You know that were merely a rehearsal for the dog to prove he can hunt. The pile of apples tumbling down was the culprit, not him.' Ned slammed his cup down. 'Tonight, we'll keep it simple – one deer for the taking. To show fairness, you can have the game all to yourselves. I'll wait till another time for my deer and you can loan the dog. Are you in or out?'

His piercing eyes challenged his gang mates to question him at their peril. They grumbled but they were in and Ned's leadership was restored.

'Will,' Ned shouted, 'more ale for Matty and Old Tom. Get yourself in here with a flagon or two.'

This seemed to lift the spirits of the room. Will appeared from the room next door with the drinks and poured out generous portions for everyone. Soon the poachers were relaxed and the atmosphere improved but shortly, with lack of sleep and full stomachs it was declared lunch was coming to an end.

'Sing us a song, Will,' cried Ned, 'before we all go home to sleep before the hunting tonight. Send us off with one of your ditties.'

Will put down the empty flagon and cleared his throat.

'I've a new one, Ned,' said Will aiming to please.

He moved a chair back and stood in the centre of the room. He loved finding songs to perform for the group. He began to sing.

'Young women, they run like hares on the mountain.'

Rufus pricked up his ears and gave a tuneful yelp. Undeterred Will continued louder this time.

'Young women, they run like hares on the mountain.'

Two strong whelps came from Rufus. And some sniggers from the men. Will was determined to finish the verse. He glared at Rufus daring him not to join in.

'And if I were a young man, I'd soon follow after.' He sang with gusto.

Rufus joined in with a long, low, wobbly cry, clearly enjoying the tune.

'To my right fol de diddle de ro, To my right fol de diddle dee.'

Rufus lifted his head and increased his volume to a howling crescendo. Will stopped singing. His cheeks turned pink with embarrassment but everyone else laughed and chortled.

'See, he's one of us. He thinks he can do better than you, Will. You make a fine duet,' said Ned ruffling Rufus's fur and handing him over to Matty. 'Take him to the Hall Brook tonight and grab yourselves a deer.'

Old Tom and Matty in happy mood bade farewell and led Rufus across the sedge moor grass back to their homes on the neighbouring Broad Field and so to sleep and prepare for the coming night. Stealing a deer was a task requiring care and skill and they would need to plan carefully.

Ned drained the last drops from his cup and gestured to Will to sit awhile. He was still chuckling at Rufus joining in with the song.

'You did well today, Will,' he said giving him rare praise. 'Before you leave, I have to ensure you know what is happening tomorrow.'

Will's smile faded quickly. He was flattered Ned was including him in his next bold venture but he was worried by the audacious plan dreamed up by Marie.

'Tomorrow,' coughed Ned, 'while everyone is chasing the missing deer, we will be helping ourselves to some French nobility.' He laughed at the notion of his own gang mates providing cover for his latest plot.

'Let Matty and Old Tom bring on the attention of the gamekeepers while we hunt the real treasure.' He curled his mouth and nodded.

'Marie says the Count will take a secret passage from the Hall to a chapel. She's heard them talking at the Hall. Every Sunday they go to prayers and the highest born sits on the Gospel side. They don't take guardsmen or weapons being a holy day and because it is St Giles's Day today and they're celebrating, she reckons it will be the Count alone making the journey while the others sleep late.'

'But how can we capture him? There will be just us and Marie.'

'Don't worry about that, I have a plan. If it's the Count alone, he will take the long way back to the Hall over the Stone Bridge – that's where we will strike.'

'And where will you keep him till they pay the ransom? We can't keep him at Sedge Moor.' Will was leading up to his contribution to the plan. 'My idea would be to keep him in one of the coal pits up past the fir trees. Duck pit has no mining in it right now.'

'Very good, Will, you are finding brains to think with but I've already found a perfect place – the Wellesbourne - the disused well on Sparrow Hall land.'

'That's Captain Ranworth's land! He'll be furious angry.' Will exclaimed.

Ned gave a sinister laugh. 'Yes, we won't say anything to Captain Ranworth and with him being so upstanding in the community, no one will suspect him of involvement. Our quarry will be safe there for a day or two. Just think how rich we'll be. We'll be able to leave this place and live like gentlemen in London.'

Will imagined himself in fine clothes with a large house and carriage. Absentmindedly, he put his nose into the air. He was walking through London carrying a silver cane with his head held high.

'If Matty and Old Tom succeed, we'll all be happy but if they are caught, then the only thing I've lost is that whining hound!

8 HALL BROOK

WHAT IS THIS SWING WORD?

NIAGA

Stars filled the velvety, midnight sky and glistened like the sequins on Seren's top. They blinked as their own levels of brightness and shape changed and came in and out of focus. Some patterns faded or shone like flickering light bulbs. Seren gazed at them from beneath the blanket cloak she had borrowed from Joe and marvelled at them. She remembered her Dad telling her about the constellations and some of the tales behind them. The darkness here was so dark it was easier to pick out the shapes. She shivered when she thought these self same stars had endured through time and if she were home, she could be looking at the same glittering sky, hoping to see a shooting star like she often did.

They had returned to Gill Moss farm after failing to persuade the Count and his friends they that were in danger and decided to sleep for a few hours, as they were exhausted. Perhaps they would think clearer when rested and decide the next step. Joe came up with a plan.

He led them to the Hall Brook on the Croxteth Hall estate. The brook ran through the forest where the deer roamed. It curled through the woods, passed under makeshift bridges and fed the ponds before trickling on to join other streams and the River Alt. He guessed it would be the easiest place to stalk the red deer and fallow deer, which were kept in captivity in the park. They were there for the sole purpose of being hunted by the Earl and his friends, with the permission of the king, who owned all the deer in the country. The Hall Brook provided the deer with clean drinking water.

Deer hunting was a sport that went back hundreds or even thousands of years. A hunter or a poacher would work with his hounds to flush out deer so he could have clear aim. A gifted hound like Rufus could find deer quickly before they had a chance to flee. Meat from deer was highly nutritious, its skin also provided furs but if poachers, who did not have permission, were caught, they could be imprisoned or killed.

'Did we do the right thing by not telling Captain Ranworth?' wondered Seren adjusting her position as she was sitting on damp leaves.

'Of course,' said Joe. 'If he reports it to the Earl, Rufus could be seized and gone forever. We have to try another way.'

'But what they are doing is wrong. I don't want to see any animal hurt. Shouldn't we get his advice first?' Seren argued once more. They had been discussing the plan for hours and the boys were in agreement. It was two against one.

'We've decided to try Joe's way first. We'll find out where the poachers are and offer our three gold coins from the Count to buy Rufus.' Tyus confirmed.

They sat quietly a while longer, studying the sky and listening to the sounds of the forest.

'It's too quiet,' said Joe. 'Listen, there's no noise at all.'

'Maybe the animals are sleeping,' said Seren.

'Or hiding,' said Joe.

The sky was changing too. One by one the stars disappeared behind clouds bringing a chill and darkness to the night. Another hour passed. Seren tightened her blanket round her and yawned.

'Are you sure we're in the right place? Where are the deer?'

'Shh,' Tyus whispered. 'Rustling.'

Sure enough, there was movement between the trees. A glimmer of white caught their eye before the animal appeared before them.

'Oh,' gasped Joe, 'it's the white deer. He's the only one in the park. He's a favourite at the Hall – even the Earl himself refused to shoot him. He's a rare sight.'

'He's beautiful,' Seren said as the proud white fallow deer struck a pose against the dark foliage almost like he was listening to them.

'He's come for a drink from the brook,' said Joe.

Tyus felt a memory stir in his mind of when he was trapped in the flooded swampland between the two bridges. He remembered not being able to lift his legs as he sank deeper into the reeds. He held his breath as he recalled being skewered by the antlers of a curious creature called a Yale. This unusual talking beast had saved his life. The gentle white deer with his fine antlers seemed like a distant cousin of the magical Yale. Tyus knew he could not let any harm come to the deer that night.

'Run!' he yelled at the top of his lungs.

Startled by the cry, the snowy deer darted into the undergrowth. The children gave a sigh of relief.

'I know why you did it Ty but if the poachers are nearby you will have given us away,' Seren said.

'Oh we know you're here now,' an annoyed voice growled, as Matty came marching through the bushes with his musket drawn. 'We've been stalking that deer this last hour and I had him in my sights.'

Old Tom arrived pulling an unwilling Rufus on a rough lead.

'What are you young 'uns doing here?' He dragged Rufus by the collar towards them.

'We've come to find you. We want to buy our dog back,' Joe said.
'Are you mad?' said Old Tom. 'You'd have to ask Ned. He's lent us his dog tonight but he's not here. You couldn't afford him anyways. Now be gone before I lose my temper – and if you breathe a word about this to anyone it will be bad for you.'

'Moonlight's gone. You'll never see a deer tonight.' Seren called out.

'Well, missy, we don't need to see while we have this chap.' He yanked Rufus over to Seren. His eyes were watery. Seren hugged him and patted his damp fur.

'Don't worry Rufus, we'll have you back with Joe soon.'

Rufus gave an understanding whine before he was dragged away again. The two poachers pushed past them and headed deeper into the woods.

'What can we do now?' sighed Tyus. 'Ned isn't with them tonight.'

'We might not have to do anything, listen,' said Seren.

The sky had filled with grey green clouds obscuring not just the moon but every star too. There was rumble of thunder some distance off.

'There's a storm coming. We'd better get out of here to safety,' said Joe.

'It's approaching fast, let's go,' Joe gathered up the blankets.

The friends found their way to the edge of the forest and the open road that led them back to the farm. The first large drops of rain splattered on their heads and necks. The drops felt strangely warm and heavy.

'This be a curious weather day, ' Joe mused, 'fog in the morn, sun in the afternoon and thunder at night.'

They were near the barn when they saw the lightning flash across the sky, illuminating the landscape. It flashed three times before it was followed by booming thunder and masses of intense raindrops. From the shelter of the barn, Tyus and Seren could see the forest that surrounded Croxteth Hall illuminated by the lightning.

'What do you think is happening in there?' asked Seren.

Joe sat on the dry hay bales and smiled. He shook off the wetness from his trousers.

'There will be no deer hunting tonight for sure. The lightning will have scared the deer into taking shelter and Old Tom and Matty would have given up for fear of being struck by a thunderbolt.'

'We might not have Rufus home yet but tonight I think we saved a deer,' Seren answered.

Tyus smiled too. He hoped the white deer found his way to safety. As Seren spoke the lightning lit up the sky once more. The thunder crashed and a silhouette was framed in the doorway.

Rufus!

9 STONE BRIDGE

ANCIENT CEASAR CIPHER CODE (-2)
e.g. When c = a, d = b etc.

WHAT IS THIS WORD?
h t g g

cdefghijklmnopqrstuvwxyzab

abcdefghijklmnopqrstuvwxyz

T he Count of Artois rose early before dawn, as he always did. He had slept soundly through the night, unaware of the thunder and lightning storm. His servant had warmed water for him in a washbowl and placed it carefully on the oak table next to the Count's bed. Furthermore, he had laid out clothes for him to wear – his silk shirt with the ruffled cuff, his top frock coat of rich blue velvet and his brocade trousers. The Count buckled his black leather shoes over his finest silk socks and stood before the mirror.

It was very important, he decided, that he dress like the aristocrat he was. He might be exiled in a foreign country, his own subjects may be calling themselves citizens these days and allowing themselves to be led by an upstart called Napoleon Bonaparte but he had faith the monarchy would be restored in France. It was possible one day he would be called to be king after his older brother. He must remain strong and alert.

Mais oui, but yes, he had joked about the peasants but he was wise enough to realise, even if he was made King, the country had changed. The peasants now had a charter called the Rights of Man, which gave them freedoms, which could not be reversed. He wanted to win back their loyalty as he said many times – he was here to repair not demolish.

It was also important for him to attend Mass at the secret Little Church Capela, as he called it, hidden in the loft at the dairy farm. Often, on the many times he had visited the Molyneux family at Croxteth Hall, he had travelled along the secret tunnel from the Hall to Gill Moss farm with a lantern. The priest or servant would be waiting his arrival. He would sit in the pew on the side where the priest would read from the Gospel scriptures and he would pray for his country, his people and himself.

Today he was alone, as Marie had predicted. The Duke of Berry and the Baron of Rolles were sleeping late after the long feasting on St Giles's day. He did not mind for this allowed him to feel more special that Mass was being celebrated for one member of the congregation – himself, the Comte d'Artois.

Afterwards, he exchanged a few words of thanks with the priest but it was too dangerous to linger, so he made his way to the Hall the long way, over the park stile and on to Hall Lane across the Stone Bridge.

It was past dawn and the sun made a sheepish appearance on the horizon. The day was going to be fine and dry though the moistness of the previous night hung in the air. The Comte liked the smell of wet autumn leaves. It reminded him of his vast parkland in France. The brooks had been replenished with fresh water from the overnight rain and the birds flew high above the pathways feeding on the breeze. The Count felt refreshed.

He would make a good king, he thought. He could unify the country and win the love and respect of his people once more. He was the chosen one to reign over France – the nobility and the peasants would bow to him once more.

And here yonder was a chance to show how virtuous he was.

A young, peasant girl, sitting cross-legged by the stone bridge, raised her palm towards him.

'Alms sir, alms for the poor. Spare some coins for this poor creature, I beg you,' she cried.

It would be uncomfortable to pass by as she blocked the bridge and although there was not a soul about to witness his generosity, the Comte was intent on finding a coin or two to give her. Indeed he could tell the story to the others at the Hall later, over lunch and they could marvel at how good he was.

'Here child, some alms from the Comte d'Artois,' he announced grandly as he bent towards her.

Instantly, she sprung to her feet and threw back her cloak. She was holding a musket in her other hand and directing the gaping barrel into his face. Before the Count could do anything, Ned and Will emerged from under the bridge. Ned carried another musket and Will some ropes.

'Hold your hands up, your lordship,' Ned ordered. 'Tie him up, Will. Well done Marie.'

Marie threw the pennies to the floor.

'Keep your change!' She snarled.

Will nervously pulled the Count's wrists behind his back and shakily tied the ropes tight.

'What are you doing?' gasped the Count. 'I am a guest of Lord Molyneux, Earl of Sefton, and under the protection of King

George III. You are in the greatest of trouble.'

'Now now, we'll treat you well – very WELL.' Ned laughed at his own joke. He was thinking of the disused Wellesbourne well where he was intent on taking the Count.

'Release me at once, imbecile,' the Count protested but to no avail.

They dragged him along the road, Ned prodding him with the musket, until they reached the end of the roadway. Here the land became fields and hedgerows again. Soon, they were crossing the Sugar Brook, which marked the boundary of Captain Ranworth's land, Sparrow Hall.

'Keep an eye out for the Captain or any of his workers,' hissed Ned. 'We're nearly there.'

They frogmarched the Count across the stream without stopping. The water was waist high and fast flowing, splashing up their clothes against their chests but still they kept on to the other side. Beyond a thicket of trees, the reached the old disused well Ned had spoken of. The well was dusty and deep but no longer contained water.

'Peasants!' shouted the Count. 'You have one chance left. Untie me or the consequences for you will be severe.'

Ignoring him, Ned removed the Count's buckled shoes and threw them to one side. Ned bundled him on to the well wall. The old rope that had lowered the bucket into the well still remained. It was frayed but Ned took a chance.

'Hold this, your Excellency,' he mocked.

The Count took hold and Ned pushed him down into the well until he landed on the rocky well floor. Ned immediately hauled up the rope to the top minus the Count. He leaned over the wall and saw the small figure of the Count glaring back up at him.

'There will be consequences!' he repeated. His words disappeared into the walls.

'No one can hear you,' growled Ned picking up the soft leather shoes. 'You'd better save your breath and hope they pay a ransom for you.'

Will dropped a rotten apple down the well. It plopped onto the count's head. They heard a whimper.

'Here's your breakfast,' Will cried and they all laughed.

'Keep a hold of this shoe Will,' Ned said approvingly. 'Keep it safe.'

He brushed off the soil from the other shoe and gave it to Marie.

'Now Marie, take the other shoe to the Earl and say we want money or this Frenchman won't be making it back for dinner.'

10 SPARROW HALL

My first is in dark but not in light,
My second is in tunnel but not in sprite,
My third is in Frenchman,
My fourth is in fur,
My fifth will tell you, I am no cur.

◆ ◆ ◆

Rufus had run to Joe and knocked him flat on the hay bale. He sprawled across his chest and licked Joe's face while Joe hugged him tightly. Tyus and Seren joined in with pats and hugs. Rufus was soaking wet from the rain but it didn't matter – they were reunited.

The dog shook off the water from his fur, twisting his body from side to side, splashing the barn and everyone in it. They giggled as they tried to dodge the droplets. Within moments Rufus was almost dry but everyone else was soaking.

Joe led the way across the cobbled farmyard and into the warm farmhouse kitchen. The children dried themselves and sat quietly while Joe found some bread and cheese in the larder for them and some bones for Rufus.

'Farmer Langley will be sound asleep by now, not even a storm wakes him,' Joe assured them.

Soon, having eaten and weary by the evening, they all fell asleep.

When morning came, the rainstorm had long gone and a chilly brightness followed. Seren was the first to wake. Tyus and Joe were sleeping either side of Rufus. Suddenly, she remembered the plan to kidnap the Count and wondered if it was too late to stop it. They had Rufus with them once more but she felt the reason why they had been drawn back here wasn't over.

Tyus blinked himself awake as if he were having a disturbing dream.

'I've just remembered – they're going to try to kidnap the Count today.'

Joe sat up with Rufus. He rubbed his eyes.

'We tried to warn him. Maybe he stayed at home,' Joe mumbled.

'Then we have to find out. We're going to Croxteth Hall again and this time we are speaking to the Earl,' said Seren. 'He'll know what to do.'

'Or should we inform Captain Ranworth?' said Joe.

'No, Seren's right,' Tyus said firmly. 'This time we must go to the Hall. We'll waste too much time trying to find the Captain. If Seren thinks the Count is in danger we must trust her.'

Seren's eyes twinkled. It wasn't often Tyus spoke up for her.

They got ready quickly. Joe gave Rufus some breakfast and the children each had an apple and some milk. All was quiet at the dairy as they set off once more past the windmill and willow tree, along the stony path, over the stile, past the Alt River and over the Stone Bridge. Ahead, the Dog and Gun was bathed in golden, early morning sun. There was no sign of revelers from the night before and it was too early for most people to be awake. Soon, the Hall lodge came into view on the horizon.

Tyus was wondering how would they talk their way past the gatekeeper this time. Would he remember them from yesterday when they were with Therese? Her face popped into his head as he thought of her. At first, she had seemed unfriendly and bossy – even rude. He chuckled to himself. She wasn't like that at all when you got to know her. He hoped, by some strange stroke of luck, she would be walking by the lodge and could help them – and it would be good to see her again.

But as they approached the lodge, there was no sign of her. Seren nudged him out of his daydream.

'It's empty,' she whispered. 'There's no one in there.'

Joe peeked through the window to double check.

'He must have stepped out for something.' He scanned the cramped room to see if the lodge keeper was asleep in a chair or standing behind the door. 'It's all clear.'

'Now's our chance, let's go,' Seren called.

Again Joe opened the gate as he had done so in the fog. They took the long path down to the Hall. This time they could see the meadow filled with wildflowers, the three trees clumped together by soggy ground and the longhaired cattle grazing peacefully. Turning a corner, the path dipped slightly then rose again bringing the Hall into view. It stood proudly amidst gardens dotted with shrubs, trees and ponds. The house was built of brick with stone dressings, two storeys high. Three storeys had been added on the west façade and looked very grand. The Earl of Sefton's carriage and horses were being made ready outside one of the entrances. Servants in livery were scurrying back and forth. Some fine gentlemen, dressed in long coats and boots, gathered together talking loudly and agitatedly.

'Something's happened,' said Seren.

'Maybe we're too late,' Tyus said, 'I can't see the Count.'

'No, but there's Captain Ranworth, standing next to the Earl,' Joe observed.

Hearing his name, Captain Ranworth looked up and saw them. Servants made haste to chase them away but the Captain called out.

'No, bring them here.' He spoke to the Earl under his breath, 'I know these children and the dog – they may have information.'

William Molyneux grunted and nodded his head.

'Bring them to me,' he ordered. The servants allowed the children to pass and seconds later they stood face to face with the Earl. He surveyed the trio with a puzzled frown.

'Why are you on my estate?' He turned his huge shoulders towards them. His hat was pulled down over his forehead and his collar stood up high so only his eyes and hooked nose were visible. It was Tyus who found the courage to speak.

'Your Lordship, Captain Ranworth, we believe someone is trying to kidnap one of your guests staying at the Hall, the Count of Artois.'

Seren added, 'We tried to warn him but I don't think he thought it was a serious threat.'

'Forgive us coming here but we thought you should know,' added Joe. Rufus added a yelp of support.

The Earl flexed the leather whip he was holding in both hands.

'You must tell us everything you know for I fear it is too late.' He threw the whip to the ground and stomped away. One of the horses whinnied sensing his anger. The Earl returned and patted his neck, calming him down. The children were unsure of what to say. The Captain continued.

'One of the serving girls at the Hall found a shoe belonging to the Comte d'Artois and brought it to us. She says the kidnappers told her they want five hundred crowns by nightfall to release him. If you know more, please say.'

'This is an abomination,' spat the Earl, 'I cannot have my guests put into danger like this. The King will hear of it. It will bring disgrace to our family. Severe punishment must follow.'

'We overheard Ned, the poacher, planning to kidnap the Count on his way home from prayers so we went to Monks Down to tell the Count but he thought it laughable.' Tyus said.

Joe joined in, 'He never thought it could happen here.'

'Absolutely not,' said Captain Ranworth. 'It is one thing for poachers to go after rabbits or dream of stealing deer but this is different. The Comte d'Artois could possibly be a future king of France. This would anger his supporters and we don't want another war with France.'

'And we don't want any harm to come to him either,' said Seren, 'He could be hurt or worse.'

The Earl studied Seren carefully. 'This young lady gets to the heart of it,' he said. 'We have to find him before the poachers panic. They could flee the area and we might never find where they have hidden him.'

'Or you could pay the ransom,' said Joe.

'Never!' said the Earl, 'I do not deal with criminals.'

Captain Ranworth removed his hat and scratched his head. 'Then what can we do? Where could they be hiding him?'

'May I see the shoe?' asked Seren.

The Earl took the black, leather shoe with its shiny, gold buckle and handed it to Seren. She knelt down with the shoe in the palm of her hand.

'Rufus!' she commanded.

Rufus instantly knew what she wanted. He sniffed the shoe and the ground. Then he sniffed it once more before running off towards the long path to the exit.

'Follow him!' cried Seren. 'He has the scent.'

They watched Rufus's red golden fur disappear into the distance. He was fast as well as sure.

'Everyone aboard the carriage,' shouted the Earl. 'I'll drive.'

The Earl sat up on the driver's seat and took the reins. Captain Ranworth sat high up at the rear of the carriage to see the road. The Earl was an excellent horseman and loved the opportunity to drive. He had won many prizes racing large, heavy coaches driven by four horses, using just one hand on the reins. The horses immediately stirred and felt his control. The children stood to one side as the four white horses waited for the signal to canter. Their hooves stamped the ground in anticipation.

'Everyone!' repeated the Earl. 'Come children, get inside the carriage!'

Tyus, Seren and Joe climbed aboard the green, velvet seats of the luxurious carriage. Seren held on to the side grabbing the smooth cloth at the corners. A servant slammed the door shut just as the Earl cracked the whip and his horses sped off to catch Rufus.

They bumped along the path and caught sight of the hound in the distance. Rufus had reached the lodge and raced under the gate without stopping. He barked to alert the lodge keeper who was staring from the window.

'He's taken a right turn,' shouted Captain Ranworth above the noise of the wheels.

The lodge keeper came running from the lodge and saw the carriage fast approaching. He desperately fiddled with the latch to release the gate, as the Earl showed no signs of slowing down.

'I told you,' yelled Joe. 'Now you know why he is called Lord Dashalong.' He bobbed on the springy seats laughing but also alarmed at the speed.

Tyus and Seren gripped hold of their seats tighter like they were on a fairground ride and being tossed from side to side.

'We're going to crash into the gate,' said Tyus looking from the window. 'Hold on!'

The children braced themselves for impact. Seren peeped between her fingers to see the lodge keeper lift up the gate in the nick of time. They careered past him at break neck speed. Her relief was short lived as the Earl turned the carriage a sharp right and raced after Rufus and they all landed in a heap on the carriage floor.

'That was close!' Tyus said as they scrambled back up onto the seats. The carriage sped ever onwards, magnetically drawn towards Rufus. He led them past the Dog and Gun and paused briefly on the Stone Bridge. The Earl drew the carriage to a screeching halt and everyone flew backwards then forwards and sank to the floor again.

'Has he found something?' they heard the Earl shout, barely out of breath.

Rufus surveyed the road either side of the bridge and sniffed the ground. Then he leapt off again having regained the scent.

Captain Ranworth muttered, 'Where's he going now?' and Joe yelled, 'Follow him!' from the carriage.

The Earl took up his whip again and cried out to the horses. With a crack they cantered off once more in hot pursuit of Rufus.

He was in plain sight and the Earl followed at a steadier pace until they came to the Sugar Brook. Rufus splashed across the stream until the water reached his neck. Then, keeping his head above the water, he swam urgently to the other side and into a copse. The trees were planted close together so it would be impossible to see what lay beyond or take a carriage through.

'This is your land Captain Ranworth,' said the Earl as the horses pulled the carriage over the brook.

'Keep going,' urged the Captain. 'I want to see if Ned has the nerve to invade my property.'

'This man has the audacity to hold my guest, a man of noble blood, against his will,' the Earl of Sefton growled.

Upon reaching the trees the Earl drew the horses to another halt and leapt from the driver's seat like a hare in springtime.

'We must go on foot from here.'

The Captain tied the horses to a tree trunk and looked in the carriage window.

'Children, you must remain here. We do not know what dangers lurk inside the forest.'

He ran off to join the Earl who was striding through the trees after Rufus.

'I'm not waiting here,' wailed Joe once Captain Ranworth was out of sight. 'I want to see if Rufus is all right.' He jumped from the carriage. 'You two can stay here.'

Tyus and Seren climbed down too. 'We've come this far. We have to see it through. We're coming too.' Seren said a little upset that Joe would go without them.

'Let's walk slowly though and stay close,' warned Tyus.

They wove their way carefully through the thicket. They could hear shouting and barking ahead.

Rufus had led the Earl and the Captain to the Wellesbourne well where the Count was imprisoned but it was being guarded by Will and Ned with muskets. At the sight of the Earl, Will immediately raised his hands into the air and dropped his weapon but Ned defiantly waved his musket in the Earl's direction.

'Take cover!' Tyus pulled Seren and Joe to their knees when he saw what was happening. 'Don't go any further.'

The Earl bellowed. 'You won't get away with this. You will be hunted down all your life. Give yourselves up.'

'Now, your Lordship, if you'd only obeyed and brought me the ransom none of this would be happening. It is your own fault.' Ned bluffed.

Will was worried. 'Ned, let's run while we can, come on.'

'I'm not the running kind Will, you know that. As I said Captain, your Lordship – it's yourselves have the blame.'

He drew up the musket to fire but Rufus leapt on him. The gun flew out of his hands firing a bullet into the ground. Rufus's teeth sunk into Ned's arm and latched on while Ned screamed and tried to prise him off.

The Captain picked up Ned's musket and pointed it at Ned.

'Good dog Rufus, you can let him go now.'

Rufus released his hold. Ned writhed around on the floor clutching his arm in pain.

'Treacherous hound!' he cried.

'You would be wiser to say nothing more to the dog and stay still Ned,' said Captain Ranworth. Rufus growled his agreement.

At the same time Will was raising the rope into the well, tugging at it slowly. The Earl stood over him menacingly.

'He's down the well, your Lordship, he's not been harmed.' He heaved the rope with all his might. 'It were Ned's doing. I had no part really.'

'Keep pulling!' ordered the Earl searching the darkness of the well for signs of life.

The Comte d'Artois was standing, the rope taut about his ankle, and slowly being dragged to the top. As he was being lifted up, he swung to and fro into the wall like a pendulum, until finally his feet gripped the sides and he could aid his escape. Soon he surfaced, shocked and grubby.

'This is an outrage,' he began but then coughed uncontrollably as the clean air entered his lungs. He bent double with the effort.

'What can we do Seren?' asked Tyus. 'It would be better if none of this had happened. We'll never have Rufus back now.'

Joe had his head in his hands. 'They'll lock all of them up, even though Rufus tried to help – it's the law.'

Seren felt in her pocket. She still had the potion Mab had given her in the Fir Tree forest. She stepped forward and walked towards the men. They froze momentarily.

What is she doing here?

Taking out the potion, she sprayed some on the Count and Will. 'Sleep,' she commanded.

Then turning to the Earl and Ned, she said the same. Tyus and Joe joined her as she faced the Captain. He raised his hand slowly.

'No, milady,' he said shaking his head. 'Not to me. I will keep the secret of what happened here at Sparrow Hall. It is not necessary to use your magic on me.'

Seren smiled.

'I know, because you are a gentleman and a gentleman always keeps his word.'

Captain Ranworth laughed.

'The potion is from Mab,' she explained. 'I can make them dream none of this happened. The Count will wake and think he is on a morning ride with the Earl, merely passing through Sparrow Hall. He will have no memory of the kidnap. I will wish the same for the Earl. He will not recall any of it. His guest is safe and he is not disgraced. Ned and Will are greedy and foolish but this time they will be given a chance. I will make them dream they must be decent men from now on or they will forever have bad luck. I will make them seek honest work in future.'

She poured the remaining liquid on to their eyes.

'They will wake soon. We must get away from here and go our separate ways.'

Rufus bounded over to Joe and licked his face.

'You are most fortunate to have a loyal dog like Rufus,' said Captain Ranworth. 'But it is impossible for you to stay here, Joe. And your friends – I don't know who you are or where you have come from but you have to go back.' He nodded his head sagely.

'There are many secrets in the world. Sometimes they are revealed, sometimes not. I will keep your secret and what has happened at Sparrow Hall forever.'

'Thank you,' said Tyus, ' but what about Joe?'

'I was coming to him. My ship sails tonight for the southern seas and New South Wales to find new plants for medicines. I think I could be helped by a young apprentice and a kindly dog,' Captain Ranworth continued. 'You will be well taken care of, like my own son and Rufus will want for nothing. Will you join me, Joe? That is my offer, as a gentleman.'

Joe leapt to his feet and clasped his hands.

'I'd want nothing more, Captain. I'm ready to go.'

'Then let us repair to my home. Sparrow Hall is less than a half mile through the trees and make ready.'

Seren and Tyus bent down and ruffled Rufus's fur one last time. They knew they had to leave. Joe had his dog and the new life he had dreamed about. Joe knelt next to them.

'Thank you for everything my friends,' he said smiling sadly.

'Take care of Rufus,' said Seren biting her lip.

'It was fun meeting you, you are a good friend,' said Tyus. 'Here, take the gold coins from the Count. They will help you start your new life.'

He pressed the coins into Joe's hand and they both smiled.

'Farewell children, safe home,' said Captain Ranworth. 'The others are waking.' It was true. The men were beginning to stir. 'Go quickly and thank you.'

Tyus and Seren ran through the copse and on to the open road once more. The Captain, Joe and Rufus took the route to Sparrow Hall. It wasn't long before Tyus and Seren retraced their steps back to the farm and the barn. The tunnel entrance was glowing behind the hay bales, lighting up the abandoned milk churns and the way for the brother and sister to return home. In less than a minute, they could see the steps to the Mill.

'Look ahead – the trap door,' said Tyus. 'It's our house.'

Seren breathed a sigh of relief. Tyus jumped up first then helped Seren up the ladder. Their larder room was exactly as they had left it. They closed the trap door and watched in amazement as it disappeared from sight.

'We're home!' cried Seren.

'We're home!' echoed two voices from the other room. 'Where

are you?'

'Mum and Dad,' said Tyus.

The parents opened the pantry door.

'Oh great, you two have tidied everything away,' said their Mum.

'And the fire,' said their father, 'it was a false alarm. It wasn't the Village Hall at all.'

Loria wiped a wayward hair from her eyes. 'A man had been burning leaves and wood behind the hall. It caused a lot of smoke and was starting to get out of control but it's fine now. The concert is still on so nothing to worry about.'

'That's great, Mum.' Seren hugged her Mum more tightly than usual.

'We do have something to show you though,' said their Dad. 'When we were in the village, the man burning leaves said he was getting too old to look after his dog these days and would we like him, give him a new home?'

'Silly I know,' said their Mum,' but when I saw him, I couldn't say no.'

'Really?' said Tyus getting interested.

'I'll get him. I think he's just the dog for us.' said their father smiling broadly.

Tyus and Seren both felt their hearts beating loudly. Dad returned with a bright and cheerful, large dog, with red golden fur and a wet nose.

'The man said his name is Rufus!'

ANSWERS to the puzzles at the start of each chapter.

Chapter 1 *Are we not drawn inward, we few, drawn inward to new erA*

The sentence spells the same forwards and backwards. It is an example of a Palindrome. The children have been drawn back to the past.

Chapter 2 *Silent Read Earth* is an anagram. Unscramble the letters and they become *Listen Dear Heart.*

Chapter 3 The riddle to *seek.*
I'm somewhere between sky and ground, always moving away.
What am I? Answer: *the horizon.*

Chapter 4 *Deer were frightened by the noise.*
The hidden word is *'then.'*

Chapter 5 The 8th letter is h, 5th is e, 12th is l, 16th is p. The word is *'help.'*

Chapter 6   The Acrostic. Look at the final letter on each line. Together they spell

'the boy'

Chapter 7   The hidden word - *star in a T shape* which is star plus T, *'start.'*

Chapter 8   The reverse word to *NIAGA* is *AGAIN*

Chapter 9   Using the Caesar cipher reveals h t g g is the word *'free.'*

Chapter 10

My first is in dark but not in light – R

My second in tunnel but not in sprite – U

My third is in Frenchman – F

My fourth is in fur – U

My fifth will tell you I am no cur – S

They spell *Rufus*

Put all the answers together to reveal the children's quest and another secret of Sparrow Hall.

* Listen, dear heart. Seek the horizon then, help the boy start again. Free Rufus. *

ABOUT THE AUTHOR

Brenda Larkin

Brenda Larkin is a children's writer and illustrator living in Liverpool, United Kingdom. She has always loved telling stories to her children and now her grandchildren. She has been a teacher and tutor for many years and has a passion for local history. The idea that history is beneath our feet or written on our street names is explored through exciting mystery stories when modern day children travel to the past and have adventures there.

The first book in the series, the Whisperers, is inspired by the medieval history of West Derby, Liverpool with a dramatic fantasy rescue quest.

Book Two, Secrets of Sparrow Hall is set in 1798 in Croxteth/Gill Moss, Liverpool and is inspired by poaching, French kings, friendship and fairy magic.
The drawings are inspired by William Pogany, vintage illustrator.

The books have been written to be accessible to children on wide

reading levels, hoping to foster improved reading skills, independent reading and enjoyment.
Although inspired by local history, the books contain the universal themes of friendship, kindness and courage and stimulate the imagination.

Twitter@BrendaLarkinBooks Instagram BrendaLarkinBooks

Printed in Great Britain
by Amazon